DESIRES, KNOWN

LILITH SAINTCROW

SAINTCROW

DESIRES, KNOWN

For Mel Sanders, as usual.

❧ I ❧

A CASTLE

COMFORTABLE SERVITUDE WAS STILL THAT—SERVITUDE. *Pacing the stone halls that grew according to his whims, staring out into the gray formlessness when he wanted a window, turning away and continuing his aimless amble when he did not. Falling onto a bed swathed with satin or a hard rock shelf and pretending to sleep, summoning feasts laid on groaning tables or a crust of bread and cup of watery, metallic-tasting wine...well, it palled. There was only so much he could do between the summons he dreaded and craved at the same time.*

How long had it been? Surely Cavanaugh had not grown weary of his near-immortality? Surely the man had more he longed for, more he would ask? Even though Hal loathed the very idea of his current bearer, he had not anticipated waiting. Of course, time moved differently here. Outside his very comfortable prison, it plodded along at an accustomed, mortal pace. Here, though, it could drag—or there could be only a single eyeblink between the rushing noise and the drugging terror, the transition to elsewhere.

He had never thought, in all his long existence, that he would actually yearn for someone to summon him and demand the tricks, the traps, the miracles.

So Hal paced, and summoned a library of books he had already read—he could not summon more until he was aware of their existence, and that required visiting that place again.

Outside.

He played with the castle's interior, and grew accustomed to silence. His own voice bounced off the walls when he chose to scream, and sometimes—impossible to deny it—he almost wanted another's to measure it against. Any voice would have done.

He endured.

❧ 2 ❧
A DOG'S AGE

"I HATE HALLOWEEN." EMILY SPENCER PEERED INTO THE dusty glass cube, squinting against the sunshine and shoving dark curls out of her face. Growing out the mop wasn't a good time, but at least longer hair might make her ass look smaller. The metabolism slowdown of her thirties felt well underway, for all that she had barely reached them. Or maybe she was just too goddamn tired for it all, and her body knew it.

"Liar." Behind her, redheaded May beamed, her arms full of bright cloth. The Thrift-Eez on Sanderson wasn't as deserted as it could be on a Friday morning, mostly because everyone had the same idea May had prodded Em away from work with—specifically, that saving money on a costume for Gloria's party next week was a good move, and that she'd probably find stuff she could wear to work as well, making it less a waste of time and more A Stab At Good Fiscal Responsibility. "Don't do witch again this year, that's boring."

"Fine. Vampire it is." Emily squinted. At least it was only busy, and not crowded to the gills inside the barnlike building. "There's a lot of junk in here."

"Vampire is boring too." Of course May would say that. She was the creative one. Last year she'd just written FREUD in Sharpie across the bottom of a nylon slip. With some striped leggings and a pair of fairy wings, she'd stolen the entire party.

"Everyone likes Elvira." In other words, *don't judge my costume choices.* All Em needed was a big gaudy ring or two; she could wear the long black dress she'd found, and with her hair fluffed Elvira would be simple. Maybe even a pair of those cheap plastic fangs, since she *damn* well wasn't going to be kissing anyone this year. The Celibacy Tournament was going strong, and she was looking to be the winner.

Not that any of her friends were playing, but still. It was kind of comforting to be the one everyone turned to for advice, since divorce made you world-weary. Pretty much everyone had gotten the message that she wasn't looking to get on the merry-go-round again. They were only trying to set her up with "really nice guys" about once a month, now.

"Nobody knows who Elvira is anymore." May wrinkled her gorgeous little snub nose. Even her light dusting of freckles was cute.

Emily chuffed out a laugh, swaying slightly to put her weight on her *other* foot. Heels were a pain and a half, even if she liked this pair. "You're no longer my friend." Her back was going to give her hell tonight. Getting older sucked.

"Ha. Good luck finding a replacement." May set off at a high clip for the checkout. Christ only knew what she was going to do with all the multicolored shit she was carrying. The copper in her hair was particularly aggressive today, and the bounce in her step showed no sign of ever slowing down.

It had been that way since high school, and it was a comfort to see some things didn't change no matter *how* ancient Em felt.

"You wanna get in there?" An old woman in a pink vest

jingled a ring of keys. Sunshine slanting through the glass front of the Thrift-Eez turned her elderly bouffant into a cotton ball, spray-lacquered in place as she shuffled sedately for the counter, and her big blue plastic earrings swayed gently. "Gonna do a costume?"

"Yep." Em refrained from pointing out that *everyone* was, or should be if they didn't want to be caught in the last-minute crush. It was a week to the Big Night, and this early, the kids were still in school and everyone else at work. "I'm thinking a couple of big rings."

For once, May hadn't had to persuade very hard to get her to play hooky. A quick run, in and out, without crowds of shrieking kids or harried parents, and she could even go back to the office if she really wanted to.

Come on, May had groaned. *Even workaholics need a day off now and again.*

The only time May had ever gotten her stick-in-the-mud bestie to skip in high school had been senior year, on the day officially prescribed for it. May often lamented that her batting average wasn't getting any better, and Em kept telling her no amount of practice would raise it.

Such conversations were boring, predictable, and utterly comforting. There was a lot to be said for the tried-and-true.

"Oh? Whatcha going as?" She even sounded interested, this kindly old lady with her pink lipstick feathering into the cracks around her lips. Her faded blue eyes twinkled, thin lavender lines in her irises. A brooch was pinned to her vest—who wore those anymore? Just elderly ladies. It wasn't very flashy, but Em would have bet it was solid silver. Looked like an eye, too, with the old-fashioned pin stabbing it. Which was faintly gross, but there was no accounting for taste. Church ladies loved to get dolled up and work in charity concerns, and the Thrift-Eez probably provided them with all sorts of fashion as well.

Em was probably looking at her future right there. Except she hadn't stepped inside a church since she'd left home. What did non-church church ladies do?

"Elvira." Emily glanced up to see the woman's expression go blank. "A vampire," she amended. "Plus, I like costume jewelry." There it was again, the urge to over-explain. As if she needed approval from a complete stranger for her Halloween costume, even.

"I haven't heard of Elvira in a dog's age." The woman rattled behind the counter, and her hands appeared in the case, ghostly arthritic fingers with their claw-nails painted pink. "You could do it, honey. Get a pushup and some red lipstick."

Well, now, Em thought her tits were just fine, but maybe even Elvira needed some padding.

The old woman put two trays of jumbled costume rings on the glass. They sparkled, cheap paste meant to look good at a distance. For all that, they were cheerful. And the price was *definitely* right.

That was when she saw the ring.

It looked like someone had taken a slice of striated agate and glazed it, an oval that looked almost like a cat's eye. The setting was heavy, and Em couldn't decide if it was real silver or not. Which was ridiculous—if it had any value at all, it wouldn't be in a Thrift-Eez, now would it?

She touched the maybe-agate with a fingertip. Maybe it was because the display case had been sitting in the sunshine —it was strangely warm, its face a little gritty. "Huh."

The price tag said $1.50 in strong, faded lettering, blue ink and pale pink paper like all the others. It had probably been sitting here a long time. And really, Emily should have left it there, but she decided the flat glassy surface would reflect well at night and took it. There was another ring, with a giant round red glass gem, that would do for her other hand. The black dress she could take scissors to and the peach silk shell she'd found for work added up to about ten dollars, and she was actually kind of pleased, not only for the bargain but because she had decided to say *fuck it* and be Elvira no matter what anyone said. It was one baby step away from her usual witch costume, it wouldn't require a hat, and May would finally stop bugging her about doing something new.

The rings went in a crackling plastic bag with the clothes, and she forgot all about it for almost a week.

❧ 3 ❧
POINT CARRIED

AFTER THE CEREMONY, WITH THE APRONS AND ROBES WERE packed away, the sword—a real antique, sure, but duller than a letter opener for God's sake—settled carefully in its case and the swinging censer cleaned out, Peter Cavanaugh settled in the leather chair and tented his well-manicured fingers. The new members were at the celebratory dinner, and there would be plenty of business handled in the next few hours. Normally, he would be among them, shaking hands, listening, dropping a quiet word here, a bit of confidence there. There were the waste management contracts to think of, and old loony George Sanderson to rein in before too much of the open bar was poured down his elderly gullet.

The bare half-dozen men here in the sanctum, however, had business of their own.

"You can't be serious." Henry Maggs set his glass of Scotch on the burlwood table next to his own overstuffed chair. He had taken to spray tans recently, and the orange shade added an uneasy layer on his olive complexion. "*That* old story?"

"If you want to go out to Peakes End again and ask *him*,

feel free." Peter's fingertips pressed against each other, relaxed slightly. Pressed again. You could see an echo of the old man in his face, the long jaw and the nose with the slight bulb on the end. His suit was hardly rumpled, though it had been a long day. Peter waited a few beats as Henry paled, and his hazel gaze passed over each man in turn.

Henry. Bruce Vance in his off-the-rack suit, who had no business concerns but a startling facility for...other...work, so he'd been given a used car lot to run and was actually doing quite well. Tim Grosvenor, the mayor's right-hand man, rubbed at his temples, his aggressive high-and-tight feathered with streaks of gray. He'd settled his bulk on a hassock, and his long, mournful face was sallow under the electric light. Rich Greene, Dick Sampson, and Eldridge Moss completed the council. The last three were only marginally talented, but better than nothing.

And they *believed*. That was getting rare. He'd even had to haul out a Seeker for them. At least none of them had peed themselves when the concave-faced beast coalesced from the flooring and roared, a sound felt more with the chest and gut than heard with the ears.

So Peter strangled his impatience and spoke slowly, soothingly. "We traced it here ages ago. It's somewhere in the city. We can't get a lock on it until someone uses the damn thing. But there have been...signs."

"What kind of signs?" Bruce wanted to know. He had taken to trimming his eyebrows too, and it looked like he'd been spending some time at the gym. The midlife crisis was well underway, and if old Brucie didn't already have a mistress, he would be getting one soon.

Peter would bet money on it. "Do you really want me to tell you? It involved—" *Fire, and blood, and calf livers. Not to mention a live rabbit that screamed when the mallet came down.*

"No, no thanks." Bruce sighed, heavily. "The old man is sure?"

"Sure as I've ever seen him. *Someone's taken possession,* I believe, are his words." The thought of the old man's too-young face and his dreamy singsong tone as he hunched over a basin of thick, rippling red liquid full of liver chunks was uncomfortable, to say the least. "Wherever it was, it's now been sold. Or someone's died and left it to someone. Who knows? We just have to wait for it to be used."

"What happens then?" Eldridge had his bony shoulders drawn up as if he expected a punch to the gut at any moment.

Well, that spinning thing in the glass case in the foyer breaks, for one. "The the case breaks, the map is drawn, and we proceed as planned."

"How is this different from any other time he's felt it moving?" Moss persisted. "How is he sure it jumped the ocean?"

"Go ask him." The headache was beginning, pressing on Peter's temples, spreading down his neck. He wished he could rub it away. Go home and go to bed. Or even manufacture a business trip that required him to spend the night out of town. Now *that* would be welcome. "Poincare's Pendulum told him so. You've seen the pendulum itself. Want to ask more stupid questions?"

"I've got one." Henry lifted a single blunt finger. "Let's say we find it. Won't the—the thing, the whatever—fight back?"

"Only if someone other than *us* has the fetter." Peter took a firmer hold on his irritation. The old rituals were stable, and proven, and they required at least four Sophics to hold the cardinal points while the Deputy Master worked, and alternates were always a good idea. He could have been elected to the titular Headship of this city's lodge, but he preferred to step back. The Head—Brad Jorgenschumer—was out there glad-handing and stuffing his face with the catered fare. He, like all the other dumbasses who thought this was just a higher-grade version of the Masons or the Elks and their toothless old boys' clubs, had no idea. They didn't care that the floor in this priory was Carrera marble, that the hangings were lovingly restored antiques, that the entire edifice with its neoclassical lines and restrained elegance in the heart of downtown hid a secret big enough to blow the top off every media outlet's head in just a few seconds.

The numbskulls were useful, though. The network, the funds, the business—wealth had always made the Sophic Brotherhood's work easier. Not every lodge had an inner council, either. Power tended to coagulate, and the old man didn't like rivals.

"I'll bet the old man can't wait to get *that* back." Rich Greene actually laughed, his nasal little whistle of amusement made all the more irritating because of the gap in his buckteeth.

Peter's headache mounted another notch. "Yes, he can't wait. So. Our Monday meeting, as usual, here. We want to be fully charged when it happens."

"If it happens," Moss corrected, mildly enough.

"*When*." Peter did not move, but his tone sharpened. That was enough. "If anyone wants out, now's the time to say so."

They all sat still. The gas fire under the heavy, carved *bola negra* mantel sizzled in the heavy silence. On the other side of the heavy door, down a long hall, the chink of silverware and low grumble of muffled conversation drifted.

Peter's fingers relaxed slightly, then *pressed* together again. The preparations he'd performed earlier that day stood him in good stead. The whiskey in his own glass, set carefully on a thirstystone coaster on the lyre table at his right hand, trembled.

The glass lifted itself by degrees. His head pounded, and the rest of them stared. Their eyes were round, even

Grosvenor's. Every time he did something like this, he had the satisfaction of seeing these assholes, every single one of them, turn into big-eyed children staring at a movie screen.

Except this was *real*.

The tumbler floated obediently within range. His hands softened, and he curled his fingers around the chill, delicate glass. The whiskey slopped a little, but he had poured a small shot just for that reason. It made no difference. Every man in the room was reminded of what he could do—and that his skills, while considerable, were only a shadow of the old man's.

Peter Cavanaugh considered the point carried.

4

SMOOTH SAILING

EMILY SQUINTED AT THE SCREEN. THE DAMN COLUMNS JUST wouldn't add up, no matter what she did to them. "That's not right," she muttered, and tapped at the keyboard.

Her cellphone, set to her right an inch from the office phone, vibrated. Probably May, saying *where the fuck are you?* They had all planned to pregame at Butler's Yard before rolling over to Gloria's to get into costume and set up the party, but the spreadsheets were just not behaving. The reports were due in Funke's office next week, but she couldn't make them square. Everyone involved had double-checked their data—or so they said.

It was irritating as all *fuck*.

Her familiar cubicle, with its ruthlessly clean walls and the whiteboard mounted precisely level—upcoming due dates in red marker, tasks in green, and the thick satisfying lines of black slicing through the three most recent victories—was soothing. The only hint of relaxation was a volunteer from Hannah Greer's airplane plant, dangling over the left-hand wall. The angle of the long, cordlike tendril holding the tiny spiky mass of new plant life reminded Em of ikebana in a catalog, so she let it be.

Hannah had seemed surprised she didn't want it clipped off. *I just thought, since you're so neat...*

Well, yes, a tidy office meant a tidy mind, but a single damn seedling wasn't going to throw her off her game. Besides, Hannah was very sweet, and just a little anxious. She would probably mourn the damn plantling, or stick it in an atrocious pot and present it to Em as a gift. Which would clutter the desk, and that Em did *not* want.

She tried the numbers again, this time merging two reports. The discrepancy showed up in red, again, and either someone hadn't entered the payouts correctly or—

A faint shuffling noise warned her, breaking her concentration completely. Em braced her hands on her desk and rolled her chair back sharply, as if she planned to get up. The rollers hit something soft, there was a bark of pain, and Em gained her feet in a lunge, whirling to see Brett the blond office Lothario grimacing as he hopped on one shiny wingtip-clad foot.

She'd rolled right over said wingtip. Served him right—he was always sneaking around wanting to "massage your shoulders, you know, just being friendly." Em herself had warned the new girl two cubicles over about him.

"Brett?" She tried to sound surprised. "What on earth were you doing?"

His big blond meaty face creased itself up like an old man's, and he had turned red. "Oh, just..." He hopped a bit, leaning against the cubicle wall, which was not meant to support that kind of weight. Em found herself hoping it would buckle and dump him on his ass. Someone should really tell him that pastel ties were a no-no; it wasn't the nineties anymore. "Just coming to... It's quitting time, Em."

Well, it wasn't like she was going to get any more work done. "That's awful nice of you to take time to tell me."

"Yeah." He set his foot down and grimaced afresh. A few cubes away, someone coughed, loud in the hush, and Em realized it was a lot quieter in here than usual. Everyone had bugged out early, either to get home before the drunks were on the road or to become one of said zigzagging drunks. Or maybe even to get some free candy; she would bet Henry Howison, the senior office admin, dressed up and went out masquerading as a kid.

God knew he was short enough.

"Well." Brett tested his foot with exaggerated care. "So what are your plans for the weekend?" His wide white grin was practiced, his dental plan probably magnificent, but Em had noticed the smile rarely reached his cold blue eyes. He was always asking if he could bring someone coffee, but none of the girls in the office said yes.

Not more than once, anyway, since afterward he acted like you owed him the biggest favor in the world. A latte was definitely not worth that shit. And those shirts of his, ironed and starched but all the same, blue with white collar and cuffs. All he needed was red suspenders to turn into a caricature.

Em half-turned, tapping in the save commands but keeping Brett in her peripheral vision. "Oh, I've got plans with the girls." Nice and bright, not giving him any opening. "How about you?"

His grin faded a bit. "Oh, just beers, maybe at the Royal." Which was the college bar out on Maroyda, not any place a grown adult should be drinking. His face fell, the picture-perfect illustration of *lonely sad puppy*.

So it was going to be the hangdog routine. Em wasn't about to invite him along. When it came to interpersonal judo, Brett was a slimy but not really dangerous opponent. "Sounds like fun for you," she chirped, waiting for the screen to clear and everything to close. She could go back to the spreadsheets on Monday. It bothered her to leave anything this unfinished over the weekend, but trying to concentrate while he was breathing on her was *not* a fun time, and she wanted to get out while there were still a few people in the office.

A few people who were *not* Brett Sandusky, thank you very much.

"Handing out candy," Brett continued. "I bought a bunch."

Maybe he was anticipating a few slutty-costume coeds at the Royal getting taken in by free candy and a splash of expensive cologne.

The screen finally, thankfully, cleared, and her wallpaper—a white-sugar beach in Hawaii, palms leaning over and the blue sea nice and calm—showed up before she hit shutdown. Em grabbed her purse and the bag she'd stuffed her costume supplies into, and prepared herself to run the gauntlet. "Nice of you." She had to slide past him to get her peacoat hanging up at her cubicle entrance, and true to form, he didn't step back to let her do it but forced her to squeeze by, her hip brushing his low-hanging knuckles. Thank God she was wearing the wool herringbone skirt today—if it had been anything thinner he might have "accidentally" run into her again. "Better finish up so you can get out the door too." Her computer screen went blank, thank God, and now all she had to focus on was escaping at high speed.

"Yeah." He followed her out into the hall. "Want me to walk you to your car?"

She glanced down the long hall at the bank of windows. It was almost dark outside, and probably raining too. Pasting on a bright smile, she told the absolute truth. "Oh, no thanks, Brett. I'm just fine on my own." Her cell buzzed again in her hand and she glanced at it, hoping the dismissal was clear enough. "Have a good weekend!"

He watched her walk away, and Em tried to do so as stiffly as possible.

The first message on her phone was May. *We're going to Gloria's early. Where are you?*

The second was Steve. *Drive safe tonight. Call if you need anything.*

He wasn't a bad ex-husband, Em reflected. She could have done a hell of a lot worse. He was even decent about the split. Sometimes Em even wished they had made a go of it, instead of just...

No, they couldn't have made a go of it. Not once he'd opened his mouth that one night.

We could just leave.

Sometimes Em wished she hadn't heard him say that. Or even wished she'd been the type of person to agree, but *that* thought only made her feel dirty inside.

Come to think of it, she also wished someone would punch Brett right in the balls. Her conscience was clear on at least one count, though; she hadn't been that someone.

Yet.

She managed to reach the elevator without being accosted again, and from there, it was smooth sailing.

5

SEED GENTILITY

GENTILITY MAY HAVE GONE TO SEED IN EVERY OTHER PART of the world, but here it had its roots driven deep. The town's historians all knew Peake's End had been one of the first great houses built on the eastern rim of North America, and its great timbered skeleton was still in good repair. No dilapidation had been allowed to caress its walls or its stone foundation; modernity was only encouraged insofar as it buttressed what had already been built. There was no "updating" of its decor or its frowning face, and whatever concessions to technology had been made were hidden.

A shadow in one of the upper windows moved restlessly. Every other room was lit with golden electric glow—a profligate use of light—but *that* window, on the large central gable, held only a flickering glimmer. Firelight, and the bright point of a lit candle.

It was to that room Peter Cavanaugh trudged, smoothing his hands back through his dark hair. The slender, stiff weight against his lower back was not nearly reassuring enough, even if it poked him when he slouched. An age-blackened wooden door loomed in front of him, and he gave two mannerly taps.

A cheerful tenor rang out. "Enter."

Peter schooled his expression and twisted the knob. The door stuck, but a gentleman never forced such things—he lifted slightly and applied the proper amount of force, and the hinges did *not* squeak this time, thank God.

The old man hated squeaking hinges.

"Ah, there you are!" He was in a good mood, maybe. The old man sat in his usual chair, his pale, effeminate hands laid along its arms. His ankles were not crossed, and he had changed out of his bespoke suit and into a smoking jacket, its velvet sleeves almost rubbed through around his sharp elbows. His hair was longer than a businessman's should be nowadays, but he wasn't in *business*. That was reserved for Peter, whose childhood had been spent in this cavernous pile. Getting the old man to agree to a heat pump instead of the fireplaces had been a chore and a half.

The old man didn't have anything against progress, *per se*, but he did not like workmen about the house.

"Good evening, Grandfather." The wooden floor creaked a bit underneath—the entire house was a symphony after sundown, groans and whispers in every hall. In his boyhood, there had been hot water bottles to keep his little feet warm at night, and the daily lessons. To step from the modern world of shiny black limousines and clunky but efficient computers into the hushed dimness of his grandfather's house where teatime was strictly observed, ancient gas-lamps still sprouted from the walls, and leather-bound tomes older than America itself gave up secrets of the energies beyond human perception was...confusing, to say the least. Resolving those paradoxes had required a great deal of time and no little agony.

Those white, spidery fingers twitched against the brocaded arms. Even the first finger of the left hand, a withered stump, twitched a bit. "Good evening, Peter. I trust the ceremonies went well?"

"As well as can be expected." To say anything else was to risk ire—a gentleman did not brag, nor did he complain. He crossed to the ancient sideboard, the decanters that were allowed a certain amount of dust—since the old man didn't want a maid in here touching things—glowing mellowly. "The inner council is growing a little restive."

"I trust you gave them a demonstration." The old man's voice was, really, very much like Peter's. The inheritance ran strong. It wasn't Peter's fault that it had skipped a generation.

"I did." And it had given him a blinding headache, one that still lingered, wrapping its bony claws around his nape and squeezing. "Theatrics are not gentlemanly, but what can one do?"

"Good boy." At least the old man sounded amused. The amber liquid in the decanters was much less than it had been this morning, but that was no indication. In some cases, the alcohol could make working the invisible easier, lowering inhibitions and pushing aside the rational mind's pointless babble. "I have been at the pendulum all day. It *has* changed hands." Those flour-white fingers twitched again, as if they felt something malleable underneath.

Great. He'd never seen the old man so worked up. Maybe the ring would be found, just in time for Halloween. Had it been sold in a garage sale? Wouldn't that be ironic—a supreme treasure of the unseen, locked in Grandma's attic for years. It was a miracle the damn thing hadn't been dropped into the middle of the Atlantic during passage.

Or maybe it had been, and Peter could look forward to his father's fate—a punishment meted out as much for disbelief as for the unhappy fact of a rationalism that would not let him believe the old man's darker mumblings.

"You're thinking about your father." The pleasant tenor shifted, grew darker. "He was weak, Peter. You are not."

Asking himself how the old man *knew* was useless. There was no point in lying, either. "Yes." A cautious answer.

But not too cautious.

The sharp, slim weight at the small of his back had grown a little damp. Or rather, it was his skin against the sheath that had done so. It wasn't that his father had been weak. It was that his father had committed the Old Man to Larkhill, and *that* had been a major strategic *and* tactical misstep.

The official cause of Henry Cavanaugh III's death was coronary thrombosis. Money spoke, even when a man was strangled by invisible hands and his wife suffered a breakdown, raving about the Devil. The entire episode had lasted six months, all told, and Peter had only been fourteen. In return for discretion, Larkhill accepted a generous charitable contribution—and Peter's mother, who passed the rest of her short unhappy days sedated into near-catatonia because otherwise she would begin to scream until her voice broke and claw at her own face.

He poured himself a few fingers of Scotch and turned. The other chair set before the fireplace was newer, and not brocaded. A simple, stern, high-backed leather club chair, its finish gleaming mellowly as the fire leapt and collapsed on itself, a brief flash of gold. Peter settled himself gingerly and only then dared to look at the old man's face.

The old man was smiling, and that was good. The pockmarks on his cheeks from childhood illness were barely visible in the dimness. The tip of his nose with the Cavanaugh bulb glowed a little, though, peeking out of the brocade chair's shadow. "It will not be long now," he said. "And when I have it again, you'll see some wonderful things, Peter my boy. Such wonderful things. I've had a lot of time to think about what I *should* have done with it."

Peter Cavanaugh restrained himself from remarking that hindsight was twenty-twenty. You could never tell when the old man would understand a modern turn of phrase and take offense. He'd been growing sharper of late, re-engaging with the world. Once or twice, Peter had come home to find the television in the billiards room on. Once to cartoons, a few times to CNN. Mostly, though, to the History Channel.

It was enough to make him wonder, and that was when he went looking for a weapon. A *real* weapon, one you could kill the unseen with, not anything so inelegant as a gun. Firearms wouldn't work, Peter knew as much.

His mother had tried.

For now, Peter arranged his feet properly and smiled. "I never get tired of hearing you list wonders, Grandfather," he lied.

The old man, mollified, began to speak.

❦ 6 ❦

FRESH OUT OF IDEAS

GLORIA HAD GONE ALL-OUT, EVEN GETTING A DJ. THE throbbing noise was consequently too loud to think through, but at least in the smaller bathroom—festooned with cotton cobwebs and black guest towels embroidered with silvery skulls—there was a little insulation from the pounding.

"Brett wanted to come along." Emily leaned over the sink; the eyeliner needed a steady hand and closeness to the mirror. "I'm sure he remembers you fondly."

May's grimace was a sight to behold. True to form, she'd come up with something great—everyone old enough to be here was old enough to remember Rainbow Brite, and the wig of yellow yarn was a stroke of genius. "Wish I *had* kicked him in the nards."

"Hah." The rings sparkled just right, Em's hair was behaving, and she'd finally found a shade of red lipstick that didn't make the rest of her look yellow by comparison. A little glitter on her décolletage and she would be ready to go and get blasted and forget about the work week. The eyeliner smeared, but that was okay. You were supposed to look raccoon-eyed—it was part of the charm. Plus, Gloria had strung red Christmas lights all over her tiny house, so the light out there was a blood-colored glow, kind to every complexion. "Steve texted too." There were lines beginning at the corners of Em's eyes, no matter how much she moisturized. "Telling me to drive careful."

"As if we're not going to spend the night in Gloria's bathtub." May's laugh, bright as a new penny, bounced off the mirror. She bent, adjusting her garters with fussy, delicate care. "He's a nice guy."

"Yeah. Just not husband material."

"True that," May agreed, loyally. She'd never asked *why* Em wanted the divorce, though she was probably dying to. "Come on, let's go out and get hammered. Gloria said something about strippers."

"Oh, for God's sake." But her costume wasn't going to get any better, and with May's legs pretty bare to mid-thigh—Rainbow Brite had never worn fishnets, but some creative leeway was acceptable—nobody was going to be looking at Em. As usual. "Okay. I'm ready. Let me just put my bag in the bedroom."

THE RED RING WAS IRRITATING, CATCHING ON EVERYTHING. The other one, glittering sharply even in the dim light, was actually comfortable, hugging her left third finger—the only one it fit, weird to feel warm metal there again—and not as heavy as it had first seemed. Three Solo cups of May's Patented Jungle Juice later, nothing in the world could have brought Emily down, even when there was a hammering at the door and the strippers showed up. Waxed, throbbing manflesh was nice—there was even a cowboy one who was sandy-blond and stacked broad in the shoulder, just how she liked them—but Em had to retreat through Gloria's kitchen because her head started spinning and if she was going to throw up, she *really* wanted to do it somewhere other than the living room.

Or on the cowboy, who had picked a spot right in front of May on the couch and was gyrating with good-natured abandon.

Gloria's deck was a jungle in summer; in winter, the wisteria vine died back and it looked a little bare. The porch light had a red bulb too, that had been May's suggestion. The cold air hit Em all at once, every exposed bit of skin roughening up into gooseflesh. The sudden shock settled her stomach, but she leaned over the railing anyway, just in case. Drunk could sneak up on you with little vomit-soaked cat feet.

I'm getting old.

The thought almost made her laugh—May would say she'd been old since she was *born*, along with boring, responsible, and most likely to have an actual savings account with something in it.

Which wasn't bad. Em blinked several times as the postage-stamp backyard blurred. The weather report had said rain, but so far it was holding off. Clear and chilly, the night was alive—running feet, children's voices, flashlights bobbing along the sidewalk over Gloria's back fence. The high, narrow townhouse was in a good neighborhood, and even though the music was loud tonight, the neighbors probably didn't mind. A leafless elm stood sentinel at one corner of the fence; Em took a cautious step sideways so she wouldn't yark into the barbecue.

The trouble was that she just couldn't get drunk enough to loosen up. There was always that little voice in the back of her head, warning, admonishing, snarking away. It wasn't even a parental voice—it was just something Em had been born with. Mom called her an overachiever—when she called at all —and Dad was, well, Dad, retired to the golf course and the

Elks Lodge instead of absent at the mill all the time. All he'd ever wanted was a son to sit and tell lies about baseball games with.

Instead, what he'd gotten was Em.

Christ. She was at a bouncing party, there were strippers inside and plenty of booze, and she was thinking about her *parents*. Alcohol was a depressant and she was probably heading that way anyway, but for *once,* couldn't she just enjoy herself?

Just when Em was sure her stomach wouldn't precipitously unload its cargo, the door banged open and out tumbled a breathless four-legged tangle. They almost went down in a heap, recovered with a lurch, and Em blinked. It was Andy and Bert, and they were both not only drunk but amorous as well. Bert, with an aggressive flourish strange for such a short, skinny hipster, pushed Andy back until they both hit the railing right where Em had started out, and she stepped hurriedly around a stack of four folded-up chairs for summer porch-parties, into the shadows next to the flung-open door.

Andy tipped his dark head back and moaned, his mouth wet and loose, dark curls bouncing. He'd come as an unshaved Blue Man, and the little bobbles attached to his headband jerked and spun wildly. Em's eyebrows threatened to nest in her hairline—Omar was inside, she'd seen him fiddling with one of the speakers just before her stomach had begun complaining. What he would think of his best friend mauling his boyfriend was a subject neither of them seemed too concerned about.

These are the situations never covered in listicles. She tried to think through the now-pleasant spinning of her poor head. *I just have to wait for my liver to process all this.*

Unfortunately, her liver was fresh out of ideas, and she couldn't get around the door to slip back inside.

So she crouched behind the stack of chairs, wincing a little as her back reminded the black platform wedges, while pretty boss at making her taller and giving her stride some sway, were not the best shoes for squatting, and cleared her throat.

Loudly.

The response was energetic, to say the least. Andy peeled himself away and whirled, too quickly for his own alcohol-loaded perceptions to keep up. He tripped over nothing and sat down, *hard*, his teeth clicking together and the whole deck rattling. Bert let out a high squeaking *"Jesusfuck!"* that might have been funny in another situation, and both of them stared, blinking, at the dark corner. Em held perfectly still. The glitter on her tits might give her away, but maybe the shadow over here was deep enough.

Well, it was Halloween, and she'd just performed a trick without meaning to. The treat would be in not vomiting or being caught eavesdropping.

"I heard someone," Andy whispered, sitting on the deck with his legs splayed and his face contorted with pain.

Bert stared, his eyes round as a three-year-old's. Could he see her? Em's lungs burned from holding her breath, and a jungle-juice scented burp threatened to give the whole game away.

The awkward silence stretched, and Em's lungs were just about to tell her to fuck off and die, when a shadow passed through the door and boots clicked on the deck. "Hey," said an unfamiliar voice. "Anyone got a ligh—oh, hey. You okay?"

It was the cowboy stripper, back in his jeans with sewn-on chaps and Velcro tabs. His oiled chest and broad shoulders gleamed, and he had the hat back on. A cigarette hung between his lips, and Em's legs began to ache-shake in that particular way that meant she was going to fall over. Crouching in heels was hard on the quads.

Cowboy Stripper offered Andy his hand; neither of them had a light. "There's, uh, matches in the kitchen," Bert said, and scurried off as if he was going to get one. Andy followed, dusting off the seat of his leotard, and Em finally let out a long soft breath, the dark speckles in her vision going away once she could fill her lungs again. The cowboy stepped up to the railing, looking out over the backyard just like Em had.

She eased upright, quietly, and decided now was a really good time to learn how to ninja-foot in heels. Unfortunately, the first step was a little wobbly. Her hip hit the stack of deck chairs, and the stripper jumped visibly.

"Jesus *Christ.*"

"Nope. Just me." Em held her arms out. "Don't shoot, cowboy." *Holy crap. Did I just say that?*

"Hey." He grinned under the hat's shadow, a nice strong chin and just a touch of stubble. "It's Elvira."

At least he was old enough to know who that was. Em was actually feeling charitable, and opened her mouth to thank him. What came out instead, though, was different. "I thought strippers didn't smoke."

The smile didn't go away, but she got the idea it was a little less real. His hand stopped halfway to his mouth, with the unlit smoke pointing at her. "Why not?"

"Well, it's a pretty athletic vocation." She didn't even slur *vocation.* She was doing really well and her stomach was settling down. Now she wanted some potato chips, nice and salty and crispy. Alcohol hunger always fastened on party foods, just like hangovers always wanted Tex-Mex. "Lots of c-cardio."

Well, fuck, that sort of blew her cool, stuttering over *cardio.* Great. This guy was probably thinking she wanted to throw herself at him.

Emily decided, with a great deal of relief, that she was not nearly drunk enough to do so.

"Yeah. You're right, I should quit both. I'm Jake." He offered the hand that had the cigarette, realized what he was doing, and laughed.

"Emily. Nice to meet you." Em edged around the stack of chairs, *not* offering her own hand. Maybe interrupting whatever booze-fueled mistake was going to happen out here had been her good deed for the night, and she could find a quiet corner. Or call a cab. May would party until dawn, but Em was already regretting this. She suspected she'd regret a lot more tomorrow when her body decided to take vengeance on her partial poisoning of it. "Good show, in there. It was really...yeah."

Then she could have smacked herself. What was the right way to say, *I appreciated the artistry of you shaking your G-string-clad package at a whole roomful of people?* Yet another thing not covered by listicles.

"Thanks." Now there was a gleam of teeth under the hat. Whether it was a smile or a grimace, she couldn't tell. "I thought I'd take a break while Rico was in doing the Latin Lover set. One of your friends is doing limbo."

Probably May. "Yeah, that sounds like something they'd do."

"So why are you out here?" He even sounded interested, those sandy eyebrows going up so hard they tilted the hat back.

Her eyes had adapted by now. His almost-stubbled chin was very nice, too. "I thought I was going to hork and I didn't want to get the carpet dirty."

He tipped the hat further back with one finger—Christ, he had all the moves, probably from watching *Bonanza* as a kid—and examined her. "Polite."

"Yeah, well." She decided she wasn't going to fall over and took another step, congratulating herself when she didn't hit the chairs again. "I, uh, hope you have a productive night."

She didn't add, *with many crisp George Washingtons*. That would be too far, even though her inhibitions were probably at doorstep level.

"This is our last stop." He didn't sound regretful.

"Then you go trick-or-treating?" *Doing double duty. Get dressed up, and maybe the candy-throwing housewives will have a few dollar bills hanging around.*

"Nah, there's another party on the West Side. Place with a pool and a bunch of food." He was still examining her. "Want to come along?"

"I'm fine here, thanks." *As a matter of fact, an Irish goodbye and a cab home is starting to seem like the best idea ever.*

"Nah." He shook his head, slowly. "You don't look fine. You look bored to death."

Oh, gee, thanks. "Does that work on girls in Jersey? Because you look about that cowboy." She held up first finger and thumb, rubbing them together.

"Ontario." His grin broadened, and now it was all smile, and all real. He was probably used to charming every double-X chromosome carrier in range with that expression.

"They have cowboys in Canada?"

"At last." He lifted the cigarette to his lips, plainly forgetting it wasn't lit. "An American girl who knows where Ontario is."

"At last," she parroted. "A Canadian who doesn't say *eh* at the end of every sentence. Have fun on the West Side, kid."

That hit a nerve. "Kid?"

I feel old. She waved her fingers at him, and set off for the kitchen door. Wonder of wonders, she could even walk a reasonably straight line.

"Invitation's open," he called after her. "You look like a lot of fun."

"Don't I wish," she muttered, and promptly banged her left hand into the side of the doorway. Or at least, it *felt* like she had, and she let out a short bark of pain lost in a sudden swell of thumping music from inside. Her fingers seized up and she had to shake them out as she headed for the buffet table in the dining room. The music swallowed her whole, and as soon as she got a handful of potato chips she saw Andy leaning against Omar's broad shoulder, those headband bobbles swaying gently.

Her stomach flipped itself over again, but she had her wits about her now. Or at least, mostly about her.

It was time to go home.

✣ 7 ✣

FASCINATING CONFUSION

HAL SURFACED FROM A SWEATING TANGLE OF TENTACLES— when the boredom reached a certain pitch, even *that* form of relief was no pleasure. Soft moaning sounds trailed away as the succubi faded, wet little kisses printed on his legs and abdomen turning chilly, roughening his skin. He knelt on the bed, the walls flickering between wood and stone, and the lighting brightened, dimmed. A frown creased his lean face— what was *that*? It wasn't a summons, if the bearer had said the words he would have been pulled forth willy-nilly. The pressure mounted, his wrists and throat beating with a frantic tattoo, as if the bearer was in danger.

Perhaps his fetter had fallen into ignorant hands? But no, Cavanaugh had been part of the Sophics, the Fratres, and though that collection of men were somewhat stupid, they were not nearly enough so to let a prized possession slip away. They were, in fact, more likely to find a loophole in Cavanaugh's near-immortality and relieve him of his treasure for their own purposes.

It made no difference. One of them was just as bad as another. A moment's worth of thought had Hal dressed in the fashion Cavanaugh preferred, just in case. A fine cloak of bottle-green, a doublet to match, lace fountaining at cuffs and his ruff fine but not overlarge, breeches and hose, and shoes buckled with wide silver rectangles instead of a workman's boots. If he was to make an appearance, it should be a presentable one.

He glanced at the room again as the lighting dimmed and brightened. A rushing sound pressed against the outside walls, and the gray fog outside would be turning bloody. Perhaps the bearer was indecisive?

The tugging began, weakly, against his hands and feet. This time, Hal did not resist. It had never done any good before, and he was—impossible to deny it—actually *curious*.

He suspected a long while had passed outside his confinement, and if his current bearer was unknowing, so much the better. Working mischief would soothe his boredom nicely, and there was always a chance he could seize something.

When one was stuck fast in miserable slavery, it cheered the heart to spread the misery to one's master, and to steal whatever could be taken to adorn the walls of one's prison. It would amuse him to work Cavanaugh a mild mischief or two as well, if the man still possessed his fetter.

The tugging came again, weak but definite. It would mount in intensity, even if the bearer escaped danger by his own efforts. The terms were strict—they did not allow Hal to ignore, and for once, he did not even truly wish to. He closed his eyes and let the faint pressure take him. The familiar sense of falling, the familiar sickening chill...

...and Hal landed on hard paving with a jolt, a confusion of voices and excitement spinning around him, the smell of a damp chilly autumn night enfolding him along with a mineral reek he had never experienced in all his long years. He drew in a deep lungful, opening his eyes, and cast about for his bearer.

"Whoa." A small, light voice, very close. "Cool costume, man."

It was *not* his bearer, but a small child wearing a suit painted with some glowing material, portraying a tiny skeleton. Hal blinked. There were lanterns over the street, burning smokeless. It was too bright to be night, too dark for dusk.

Wherever he was, it certainly smelled better than usual. The thick mineral tang in the air was not nearly as bad as the usual choking pall of human excrement, smoke, and small dead animals, but it required a bit of adjustment nonetheless.

A group of children appeared, shrieking and laughing in carnival finery and masks. They swung heavy bags and babbled excitedly, dividing around Hal as a river around a stunned rock, and something very large and shining heaved past with a coughing roar. Hal flinched, the power rising to strike—but it was gone in a heartbeat, and he realized there was no danger. It was simply a sleek metal carriage, its eyes bright diamonds, going far more quickly than the horse-drawn traps of Cavanaugh's world.

What, in the name of the Ring...

The children were herded by a pair of adults who gave him strange glances. The woman was wearing *breeches*, and both of them—and all the children—had all their teeth, except one or two of the children missing only milk-fangs. They were much taller than mortals usually were, and overfed as well. Smooth skin and gleaming eyes—at least he was among the wealthy. He cast about, deciding it would be best to be taller once he had a moment to attend to his physical form.

The mortal man cleared his throat, his expression familiar. Protective, and a little wary. "You lost, Mister?"

Their speech was different. Hal's head hurt, a swift lancing pain as he absorbed its rudiments. Very close to

Cavanaugh's tongue, as a matter of fact. "Yes, lost." He chose the words with care. "I shall find it soon."

The parents—though they could not have produced such a numerous brood, the children were *everywhere*—exchanged another troubled glance, but their charges were hopping up paved steps and hurrying to the door of a large domicile. With every window lit and the outside festooned with all manner of paper and strange symbols, it could have been a castle. It would have been counted one, in the time of his early bearers.

The door opened, and the children chorused "*Trick or treat!*" The adults hurried after them, and now Hal could see the entire street was alive with mortals intent on the same business. Each gigantic house was large and copiously lit, too, with warm golden glow that did not flicker as flame would.

Intriguing. But he had to find his new bearer. He turned in a complete circle, searching.

"Ow!" A woman's voice, the sound of a scuffle. The hook sunk into Hal's belly twitched, tugging him forward, and he had no time to admire the poured stone of the walkway or the young trees flanking it. It looked very much like Roman cement, and he burned to find out what he could of this new, rich, fascinating confusion.

Perhaps he could sweeten the new bearer's temper until he had learned everything he could, then irritate them into sending him to the castle to think.

No, that would not do. The thought of going *back* was unpleasant at best. He'd had his fill of being trammeled.

Hal quickened his pace, catching a thread of unphysical scent. The bearer had come this way, and recently, too. As he walked he swelled, subtly, until he was as tall as the glamorous, rich, exceedingly stout adults hurrying through the darkness.

❧ 8 ❧

A SINGLE DROP

No children came up the drive at Peakes End. They knew better than to climb the stone wall at the end of the property, or try to wriggle through the bars of the iron gate. Even the rowdiest little snotnose stayed away, most likely instinctively. It was a variant of the same aversion thieves would feel when approaching a place the Sophics used for their ceremonials.

Well, the *real* rituals, not the mumbo-jumbo for the outer circle. And children were exceedingly sensitive before they hardened and stopped believing.

Peter had finally laid down, his head on a snow-white linen pillowcase, and let out a long sigh. The antique bed-curtains were drawn, and the stuffy, enclosed feeling of safety was a balm, especially to his aching head. The old man hadn't wanted his dinner, and Peter's own stomach was a knot.

Any moment now, the old man kept muttering. *Any minute.*

When did people stop using curtained beds? The old fossil would know, but damned if Peter would ask him. It was getting harder and harder to stay calm when the—

A muffled thud. Peter sighed, digging his head into the

pillow. If the bastard was tearing apart one of the rooms again, he could fucking well do it.

Peter's hand curled around the chilly, almost glassy hilt. Sleeping with the thing under his pillow was safer than letting it out of his sight for a single moment. If the old man suspected he was carrying it around, there would be...unpleasantness. And quite a bit of it, too.

A sharp, crinkling shatter-break sound jolted him upright. Peter tilted his mussed head, listening intently. His senses were very good, youth and the family inheritance giving him another advantage. Gym-hardened muscles tensed under his T-shirt. Sometimes the old man patted his arm and said *a fine figure of a young man*, just the way he might talk about a good horse or dog he'd bred for hunting until such things were no longer primarily a gentleman's pursuit.

"*Peter!*" A bellow from downstairs. "*Peter, my boy!*"

It was a damn good thing the staff went home every night. An even bigger blessing was that the old man barred the door to the central gable room when they showed up in the morning. *Idiots*, he would sneer. *In my time, servants knew their place.*

The unpleasantness with that one girl—Juanita? June? What had her name been? Well, anyway. That had been expensive, but not in cash. And now he knew what the old man had done to make his own daughter-in-law scream and claw at herself.

Memories like that were best kept buried.

Soon, he'd told himself. *Soon, when it's time.*

Sometimes he even dreamed of it—driving the glittering blade in, the wet, meaty sounds as it pierced ageless flesh and made it vulnerable, the expression of pain and terror on the old man's face. Would he look like Peter's father before death came? The resemblance between them had been marked, but not overwhelming. Then again, there were how many generations between him and the old man? He'd done the math once, digging through the complicated genealogy. Just now, though, he couldn't remember.

It had been a long day.

"Peter! Peter!"

Peter sighed again. Christ. He couldn't even *sleep* without the narcissistic old bastard intruding.

A few minutes later he shuffled down a flight stairs, his slippers making soft secret sounds and his dressing-gown properly tied. Peter stopped, considering the stained glass over the repaired door to the *other* room the staff was never allowed into. The noise was coming from behind it.

The study. The books were there, some in temperature-controlled cabinets, others ranged along shelves almost groaning from the weight of knowledge. The two desks were there, too, and a bay window looking out onto the garden. In the middle of the room, the glass case stood.

When he swept the door open, he saw the old man, capering barefoot on a priceless, threadbare Persian carpet. Bloody footprints swung and splashed drunkenly through shards of broken glass. The old man stopped, and Cavanaugh almost shuddered. Lank dark hair swayed, no ribbon tying it back now, and the scars of childhood smallpox on the old man's cheeks were glaring because he had flushed with excitement.

"Look!" the old man crowed, dancing on the broken glitters. *"Look! Look!"*

The case was indeed shattered. Glass had exploded outward with some violence. The apparatus inside, dust repelled from its static charge of invisible force, was something a Victorian reader of penny dreadfuls might have recognized—a brass arm, lambskin held flat on a tablet-surface, a quill with an oozing end.

A spirit-writer. All through Peter's childhood, a single

drop of gall-ink had trembled on the quill's pointed end, never falling.

Now the arm moved, a furious scratching as ink splattered, and the map was being drawn. Ink raced in streams, and the outline was recognizably their city.

The old man arrived next to him and hugged Peter, his wasted arms closing with surprising strength. His battered feet would heal in moments. "Peter, my boy!" Were those *tears*, in the old man's eyes? "Oh, my blessed boy, it's happened! We must send the Appetites! Wake the inner circle!" He took in a long, wheezing breath, and shouted again, in his great-great-however-many-times-great grandson's ear. "*Someone is using the ring!*"

❦ 9 ❦

GOOD ZING

STAGGERING OUT GLORIA'S FRONT DOOR AND HEADING FOR Twelfth Street had not been her brightest idea. That made *twice* now she'd almost tripped over a pile of little bastards out harvesting free candy from every sucker in sight. Her work shoes weren't much better than the platform boots, but she should have taken the time to sit down at the party and put them on. Now she was faced with the prospect of sitting on the curb to do it, and probably getting something nasty smeared on her dress in the bargain. It was a one-time deal of a dress, but still.

May wouldn't care, but May could look good smeared with dirt.

Em suspected there was little chance of catching a cab around here, too. She was beginning to further suspect that if she *did* find somewhere to sit, she might still be there when dawn came, because her legs were doing a shaky-weird thing and the alcohol, having left her stomach alone, was filling her head with fumes, random thoughts, and a spinning sensation that made navigation difficult, if not impossible.

"Hey!" Running footsteps behind her. Em braced herself,

grabbing at a huge plastic garbage can as she half-turned, peering down the dark sidewalk alive with kids, harried parents, and the occasional staggering partygoer just like herself.

The one jogging toward her looked familiar, and she blinked at its misshapen head before she realized it was a ten-gallon hat. It belonged Ontario Cowboy, in fact—she just hadn't recognized him with the white T-shirt on instead of the fringed vest he'd done all the dancing in. He was coming at a good clip, and that much muscle was probably hard to stop.

He almost overbalanced, as a matter of fact, and bent over to catch his breath while Emily regarded him curiously. "You really should quit smoking," she said, and the look he darted her might have been sarcastic if not for his deep, hacking sounds.

She waited, studying him, kind of glad the garbage can was there to hold onto. *I don't think I forgot anything. Why is he chasing me?*

He really was kind of cute. Those shoulders were dreamy, and she'd bet girls liked to rest their heads on that broad chest and agree with anything he said.

"Hey." He straightened, his pecs filling out the T-shirt nicely. "Look, I just...did you see that guy? He was following you."

"What, like you were?" All the same, a chill went down her back. There were a few things that could make a woman insta-sober, and *that* was one of them. She glared again at the sidewalk behind him, straining to see anything out of place.

"Not like me." Ontario Cowboy gasped again, got his breath back. He swiped the hat off, and under it he was all sandy-haired and earnest, with a cleft in the middle of his chin. "Look, just come back to the party, all right? Wait for a cab, or one of us can take you home. You were weaving pretty bad, and that guy—"

"What guy?" It wasn't any use. She couldn't see anyone who looked suspicious, and her legs fucking *ached*. A faint trace of steam rose off Ontario's muscled forearms. He was stacked, no question about it, and he wasn't doing the old *you're in danger, get in my car* routine. What he was proposing was logical, and safe, and even sound. Or at least as logical as her inebriated head could wrap itself around.

"Guy in a suit, sort of. Steampunk, maybe. He was following you pretty close. It looked wrong."

Well, wasn't this cowboy the white knight. Em blinked several times, shuffled through all her priorities, and decided on one. "Why were *you* following me?"

"Your friend in the blonde wig got worried."

Oh, May. "Christ. She should just have a good time." It wasn't like her to even notice Em had slipped away. Maybe she was growing some responsibility?

Oh, please. That'll be the day. Still, the thought was a little unpleasant. Em didn't have much except *responsible* to recommend her, and if May took that over too, what the hell would happen to her?

It was the sort of clarifying, hideous thought you had when you were too smart to express it kindly or lie to yourself, and she was just glad it hadn't bolted straight out her mouth.

"Come on. Can I at least call you a cab?" The cowboy worked at his hatbrim with both hands, like a kid afraid of getting in trouble.

She was about to inform him that she could call her own damn cab, but her left ankle buckled and she swayed, even though she was clutching the trash bin. Maybe three Solo cups of jungle juice was a bit too much.

He grabbed her arm and hauled her upright; she spilled

against his very broad—and very hard—chest. *Bro, do you even lift?* The giggles started. Here she was, clutching a garbage can and falling on a stripper.

It was the closest she'd come to May's idea of fun in years.

"Thanks." She tried to untangle herself, but ended up with her palms flat on his chest. The heat of him through the T-shirt was enough to short-circuit a thought or two. "You're right. These shoes are killing me."

"But they look great." His teeth were *very* white, and that smile had probably pleasantly devastated a few housewives. "I could carry you back. It's not far."

"You Tarzan. Me drunk." She shook her head, but that was bad too, because it made the whole world whirl. "No, no thanks. You could let me lean on you, though."

"Yes ma'am."

Good Lord. Even Canadian cowboys say ma'am.

She managed to step aside and grab his arm as another flood of kids streamed past. A little girl with an LED-flashing wand and a pink princess dress pointed the wand at them. "COWBOY!" she screamed, and shook the thing furiously.

"You have a new fan." The thought was deliciously hilarious, and laughter bubbled in Em's throat. Her ankle threatened to turn again, treacherous on the uneven sidewalk, and the cowboy put his arm over her shoulder.

"Grab my belt."

"If I had a nickel for every time..." She swallowed the rest of it—not appropriate for children. "Good God, you have a huge buckle." It had *rhinestones*, too.

"Part of the costume." A chuckle hit him halfway through the words, and that set her off. She shook with hiccupping laughter as he hauled her down the sidewalk, gaining a few disapproving glances from parents shepherding along groups of little freeloading spawn.

It took half a block for the laughter died in fits and starts, and her head was *really* whirling now. "God, why can't I just be home?"

"Tap your fabulous heels three times." He lifted her over a rise in the pavement, one she would certainly have tripped over. "Worked for Dorothy."

"I didn't know they watched movies in Canada."

"We just don't shoot people in the theaters."

"Oh, ouch." It was a good zing, and she supposed he was pretty spiffy. In fact, she supposed May had not sent him out of concern. "How much are you paid for this?"

"Helping a really hot drunk girl down the sidewalk? That's sort of its own reward, ma'am."

No, I mean how much did May pay you to cozy up to me?
"Drunk is never hot."

"I'm sure you're fun when you're sober, too."

"What was your name again?"

"Jake."

"Well, thank you, Jake. I happen to be too old for you, but I appreciate you making an effort." Her tongue was too big for her mouth, and Emily supposed she should just quit talking. Her filter was pretty much gone for the night, and the idea of telling everyone she met exactly what she thought of them, while *highly* amusing in her current state, was probably not what you'd call a Good Life Choice.

Jesus, even when I'm drunk, I'm boring.

"Yeah, well, I'm too old for this and this is my first night stripping, so we're even. I go back home in six months with my degree and a bunch of wild stories to tell."

So, he'd popped his stripper cherry tonight? She decided not to ask how he'd gotten roped into it. *Roped* into it, a good pun, it made her giggle again, breathlessly. She hadn't laughed this hard in months.

When the spasm passed, she had her next line ready. "A degree? Fancy." Gloria's house was getting closer. She could hear the music thumping out, and a yell of *Trick or treat* rode over the bass. Gloria was at the door, done up in full gypsy-fortuneteller, tossing candy by the handful into pillowcases pressed into service for the night.

Emily stopped, let go of the cowboy, and grabbed Gloria's front fence instead. Wrought-iron, older than pretty much anyone there, it was reassuringly solid. And cold. "Your very first time. Well, you looked like a pro. Good luck with all your stories. I'm going to stand right here and wait for a cab."

"You, uh, might want to call one. Or you could be waiting all night."

She was already fishing for her phone. "Good idea. Christ." She took a deep breath, a wave of shivers passing through her from shoulders to hips as she realized just how chilly it was, and she was out here without even a coat.

"I'd offer you a ride, but—"

"But I wouldn't take it." Her fingers finally found her phone. She *had* forgotten something, she realized. Her peacoat was inside Gloria's house, but she'd had the presence of mind to stuff her purse into her work bag and haul them both with her during her quest for freedom. "Not safe."

"Well, Clyde's not drunk, but—"

"Not getting into a car with a bunch of guys while I'm intoxicated, thanks." It came out *intoxshicated*, and the wavering weird feeling in her head meant she was pretty close to passing out. "'Specially a man named Clyde." *Oh, man. This isn't good.*

She was no doubt incredibly amusing, because he grinned again. "Cautious. I can understand that. I, uh..."

"Whatever." Her phone had somehow gotten tangled in the white cotton panties she'd worn to work. She pulled the whole damn wad of fabric and phone out; the mad idea of just flinging her knickers at the cowboy and telling him to go the fuck back to Ontario was so attractive she immediately clapped a lid on it. "God. I wish I was home already."

She must've had more than she'd thought, or the liquor had finally hit, or something, because between one second and the next, all the lights winked out, and there was a rushing noise.

Oh crap. Emily squeezed her eyes shut. *Please don't let me pass out holding my panties in one hand and my—*

Too late.

❧ 10 ❧

NOT TOO DEMANDING

A WOMAN. A THIN BLACK DRESS OF SOME SLIPPERY material, not as pleasing as silk, and dark, curling hair piled atop her head. Hal held the slight weight in his arms and turned in a full circle, slowly, his heeled shoes crushing strange carpeting and his head ringing slightly from his first service to his new bearer. It hadn't even required a great deal of power, just a simple jump from *here* to *there*. Keeping a mortal insulated from the ill effects of such an act required more care than the transition itself.

The ring was on her third left finger, its baleful eye glowing at him. It did not match her delicate hand—so soft and graceful, though the nails were extremely short. So she was a lady. Perhaps this servitude would be full of frivolity, and when he was ready, a woman would be easy to persuade into a fatal misstep.

It should have troubled him to consider it so calmly, but after so long chained, even the mildest of dogs might grow vicious. This place was not lit with that strange golden light, so his pupils swelled, adapting swiftly.

So this was her home. Soft, comfortable-looking furniture. A flimsy door led to a bedroom full of the scent of a healthy female, and some other heavenly odor he could not identify. Perfume? A flowering plant? There was a kitchen, a room with a tiled floor that looked strangely like a private bath *and* privy all in one, and shelves full of objects he longed to examine.

Hal carried her into the bedroom. Her bed was much larger than a maiden's cot. Perhaps she was married? But then, what husband would let his wife roam in this manner, and speak so freely to other men? The one he had spirited her away from was obviously a stranger. Their conversation had filled his head with new words, but he had little in the way of scaffolding to frame them correctly.

Soon enough.

He arranged her on the bed. All was luxury, from the heavy blankets to the carpeting, a window of very fine glass, scattered clothing in strange forms. Her shoes were held on by an ingenious little system of very small interlocking teeth arranged in a row, and they opened as he drew a metal tab down.

She made a soft sound of relief as he drew the first shoe away, her hot little foot relaxing. Hal froze, but she didn't stir, and her breathing was deep and steady. Perhaps she was a spoiled noblewoman, but what father or brother would let her behave in this manner? The world must have changed indeed while he was trapped in the castle, waiting for a call.

The second shoe came away just as easily. She rolled over, curling around her large leather bag and burying her face in soft pillows. Her ankle was remarkably dainty, her calf a beautiful soft curve...ah, the temptation. His first female bearer. Perhaps she would require a soft service or two. Cavanaugh had once or twice allowed him to wench alongside him, and despite the release, that had not been as enjoyable as he expected.

He retreated from the bower on silent feet and set out to find what fuel they used in their lamps. Once he had solved that mystery, there were two bookshelves ready to be plundered. And, he suspected, a great deal of history to digest before the bearer woke in the morning and began making demands of him.

Hal paused, something nagging at him. What was it?

Finally, reluctantly, he stepped back into the bedroom. The ring would not loosen until he had performed a direct, commanded Work for her, but he did not consider sliding from her hand. Such a thing was impossible anyway—had he tried, the punishment would have been instant, and she would not feel a thing. The fetter itself would act.

Instead, Hal drew the messy, jumbled blankets up over her, his knuckle brushing the curve of her hip as he settled the cloth carefully. At the very least, she had done him a service, and he could hope she was not *too* demanding.

❧ 11 ❧
WHAT KIND OF DRUGS

A FAINT, FARAWAY BUZZING NOISE. BRIGHT LIGHT STRIPING her face. Her head was being squeezed in the fist of an invisible giant, she was sweating, and she'd slept in her bra *and* hairpins.

Ugh. Em groaned, realized the buzzing was her phone. Had she blacked out? She managed to peel one eyelid up a little, wincing at the light. She groaned again, this time with feeling—what the fuck had May put in the jungle juice *this* time? It had gone down suspiciously easily, and she'd felt like she had a handle on things until the shoes started giving her trouble.

The last thing she remembered was the Canadian cowboy offering to call her a cab, and Gloria tossing handfuls of candy into trick-or-treaters' bags. Something about panties, too. Her own panties, not Gloria's.

Oh God. Did I do something May would have done?

Well, the cowboy had been cute enough. Probably too young to find the clitoris, though. They learned *that* late, if ever.

Her phone kept buzzing. Her work bag was cuddled

against her head, too lumpy to be a real pillow, and her neck had a gigantic crick in it. It took her three tries, then dumping the leather bag's contents out onto the floor before she could scoop the phone up and grimace at the familiar photo blinking on its stern little face.

She hit the *talk* button. "God, stop calling, I'm fine."

"Good morning, sunshine." May sounded altogether too fucking perky. "Nifty Irish goodbye, by the way."

Emily winced, holding the phone away from her ear. Her head felt like it was going to explode. Even the framed print of da Vinci's *Madonna on the Rocks* on her bedroom wall was too bright. "I needed to be home to greet my hangover properly."

"Yeah, well, you did a number on Jake."

"Who?"

"*Jacob*. Cowboy hat, remember? Long tall drink of Texan?"

Oh. Cowboy. "He's not from Texas."

"Whatever. Well?"

"Well what?" Emily managed to roll over, squinting at the curtains. They were wide open, and pale wintery light was flooding her entire bedroom. *Dear Past Emily, you are a bitch. No love, me.* "I think he called me a cab."

"Isn't he nice? You made a big impression."

Did I? "Oh, Christ. I have to go throw up now." Her sheets were still clean and smelled of fabric softener, which was grand except even that wonderful fragrance made her head pound.

"What? He's not bad at all, I know you like them a bit thick—"

No, they were *not* going to discuss her tastes right now. Not while she felt like this. "What the fuck did you put in the jungle juice, May?"

"Trade secret." May's laugh was only a little jagged. She'd probably already had time to drink a ton of water and take some aspirin; hangover nursing was the only thing she got up early for on weekends. "You never used to be such a light-weight. You could thank me, you know. Boy is *stacked*."

That is entirely beside the point, sweetheart. "Mrgle," she muttered, hoping the sound would pass for gratitude, and disconnected. She checked the date—yes, it was Saturday. Yes, she was hungover. She had all day to recuperate, and the first step in that was...

She sat straight up, wished she hadn't because an invisible spike went straight through her brain and her stomach sloshed. There was no doubt about it. She was smelling coffee.

Had she set up the coffeemaker last night? Drinking to blackout was not good, and if she'd even *touched* any of the kitchen appliances there was likely to be a huge mess out there.

Another groan worked its way out of her throat, and she took stock. Her legs would carry her. At least her shoes were off, so her feet weren't cramped and swollen. The dress was twisted and bunched in interesting ways, but it didn't smell as if she'd vomited all over herself. Though if she had, she would probably be feeling better right about now, since the alcohol would have been outside instead of in.

She shuffled for the bathroom, moving gingerly and hoping the coffeemaker wasn't dying. Maybe it was a scent-hallucination. Was that a symptom of liver failure?

Brushing her teeth, ridding herself of excess fluid, and getting the goddamn bra off helped, but not nearly as much as she wanted it to. There was no cup by her bathroom sink, so unless she wanted to try to slurp from the faucet she had to go into the kitchen. Water. Some aspirin. Maybe calling that burrito place on 34th that delivered, too. Her stomach rumbled a bit at the thought, caught between hope and disgust like the beginning of a second-and-last date.

Gratefully tasting minty toothpaste instead of sour bile, she opened the second bathroom door and shuffled out, rubbing at the underside of her left breast where the wire had poked unmercifully. She rounded the corner and halted, her head tilting and her hair falling into her eyes.

What the everloving fuck?

There was a man in her kitchen.

Well, *shit.*

Tall enough, though a bit narrow-shouldered, and olive-skinned. He had a nose that could have passed for architecture and high cheekbones too, dark eyes and dark hair pulled back into a ponytail—well, at least it wasn't a man-bun. He wore jeans and a blue cable-knit sweater that looked vaguely familiar, and he had his long-fingered hands up, palms out, as if he expected her to start screaming.

"*You're* not a cowboy," she blurted. And a quick internal rundown came back with the answer that they probably hadn't had sex, thank God. Still, this was goddamn awkward.

He blinked. He had great eyelashes, nice and thick. He didn't look like one of the strippers. Maybe a cab driver?

"Ah. No. I am not." He seemed a little at a loss. A faint accent behind the words.

"Great. So...did we, um..."

"What?" He sounded just as stunned as she felt. "I beg your pardon, madam, but I—"

Madam? Was he foreign? She chided herself for assuming, and decided at the same moment that candor was the best policy. "Did we have sex?"

"No. Did you wish to?" His eyebrows lifted a little, as if he either hadn't considered the option or he was surprised she'd asked. Or maybe she wasn't his type.

It was probably the latter. "Uh, no thanks. I'm trying to grow my hymen back." She folded her arms, maybe a little defensively. "So, you brought me home last night?"

A relieved nod. "Yes. I had to, because—"

Because I was shitfaced. "Okay, so you're a nice guy. Do I owe you gas money?"

"What?"

Not very bright. "What do I owe you? For bringing me home."

His hair was very thick, too. The ponytail looked braidable. If he was just a little more stacked he'd be exotic. As it was, he was quite respectable, but the priority now was to thank him kindly and move him along before he got any funny ideas.

"Ah, nothing. I believe some explanations are in—"

Well, she should start at the beginning. "Did I puke in your car?"

"What?" He couldn't look more baffled if he tried. Well, maybe he could, but it would be hard.

Jesus Christ. Well, that's probably a no. Her head gave another flare of pain, so she headed for the sink. "You slept on my couch, right?"

"...Yes. After a fashion." His boots were nice, though. The whole outfit looked familiar, but her head hurt too much to pin it down.

It was small consolation that even with her skull pounding this way, she was obviously quicker on the uptake than this random stranger. "Well, you're a good egg. Thanks. Look, I'll call for breakfast, but I need some water and some aspirin first. Unless you'd rather just boogie now."

"Boogie...now?"

Did he not understand English? He seemed to get most of what she was saying. "Sure. There's the door."

"You...wish for me to go away?" His air of puzzlement intensified. Guess she'd been wrong about just how baffled a guy could look.

"Don't you want to go home?" Her head would *not* stop

pounding. Next Halloween, she was putting on a Designated Driver badge and comfortable shoes. To *hell* with all this.

"I have no home."

Great. A homeless guy in my kitchen. Never drinking again. "Oh. You live in your car, or..." May got drunk and picked up stockbrokers or Austrian pilots-in-training. Em, the one time she really went overboard, picked up a bum.

"The ring." He pointed at her left hand, a quick sketch of a movement. "It is my fetter."

What, he wants it? "I bought it at Thrift-Eez. Buck-fifty. Cute, huh?" She filled the glass and took a long drink of water, watching him over the rim of the glass. He really racked up her weird-o-meter, but he didn't seem dangerous.

If he had been, he had every opportunity to be an asshole last night, and as far as she could tell, he hadn't. It was a close shave, and one more reason to jump on a sobriety wagon. Getting older made you risk-averse. May would no doubt call her no fun at all. But in a world where you could be shot by an ex on courthouse steps, or get your tits cut off by the 'nice guy' who brought you home, that kind of fun had too high a price tag.

He opened up his mouth, and proved he was not only weird but completely batshit. "I was bound into that ring, and now I serve each bearer to the limit of my ability. Whatever you wish for, I may provide. I am—" Here he sort of melted down, kneeling on her kitchen floor, with his back to her round silver garbage can, "—your slave."

She needed the water too much to choke and spray it all over the kitchen, but it was damn close. When she finished drinking, suppressing the acidic belch of an empty, liquor-abused stomach, she fixed him with a steady look and took a deep breath.

First things first. "Okay, dude. What kind of drugs are you on?"

❧ 12 ❧

PICKED UP FOR A SONG

THEIR BOOKS WERE FULL OF STRANGENESS. THE BLANK screen that showed moving pictures—*tele-vision*—was full of so much conflicting information it strained even *his* comprehension. He had been locked in the castle for over three hundred mortal years, and a single night spent devouring every scrap of reading material he could find while learning the use of the television and the cold cabinet for perishables, not to mention the other machines, was not enough. Apparatuses for heating food, for making coffee—just imagine that, a *woman* drinking coffee, it threatened to strain even *his* excellent comprehension.

Their plumbing was extremely efficient. The shining chariots were *cars*, and it was their metallic breath choking the air. He had passed his hands through the television, enjoying the tingles of their electricity and learning how it was made, inferring what he could not sense.

A brave new world, indeed.

The woman glared at him, clearly not understanding the import of his words. She was smaller without those high shoes, and her hair was a soft, wildly curling nest. She had wide dark eyes, a trifle bloodshot, and had soused herself thoroughly last night. For all that, she would be accounted handsome indeed in Cavanaugh's time. Her teeth were strong, and the curve of her hips was enticing. Lovely round, frank breasts—her nipples showed through the thin fabric, and there were tiny glittering specks across her décolletage.

Yes, she was pretty, in the way only young, healthy mortals could be.

He decided to speak very slowly, so she could understand. "I am not drugged." *Unless it is with wonder, to see what has been wrought in my absence.* "You wear the ring, I am your servant."

She filled the glass again. A marvel—fresh, clean water, with merely a twist of the wrist. Their sewers must be miraculous, too.

She drank, her throat moving with long swallows, then refilled the glass afresh. A prodigious thirst—she took a deep breath, and turned, her small, tender, bare feet quick and light. The dress hid nothing of her body. They were strangely forthright in all their equipage, these new mortals. Their men were children, and their women walked about without protection or guidance. It would be maddening until he adjusted.

If she did not condemn him to return to the castle with misunderstanding.

"Sure," she said indulgently. "I'm going to get some aspirin. I'll get breakfast, and then you can run along. For right now, though, get up off the floor."

As a command, it lacked a certain...something. He rose, slowly, and followed her. The mirrored cabinet in her bathroom opened, she extracted a small bottle—plastics, high-quality glass, mirrors not of polished metal but of glass itself, no end to the wonders—and, he realized, she was carefully watching him in the mirror.

So. There was *some* caution in her. That was good. He

took care not to block the door, standing further away than he wanted to. "You do not believe me." At least his *other* bearers had deliberately invoked him. It looked as if this one had not.

What had happened to Cavanaugh? The man had sent him away in the middle of his debauch.

Your expression does not please me, lying sprite. Begone until I summon thee again.

"Oh, I believe *you* believe what you're saying. I very much believe that." A tight smile accompanied the fine distinction, one that did not reach her wide dark eyes. "And if I didn't have such a headache I would love to hear more about it. I really would. You want some aspirin?"

"No." Cavanaugh should not have sent him away, but who was Hal to argue? He had known others of Cavanaugh's so-called brothers were jealous of the man's power, and it was part of his curse to protect the bearer.

He could not do so from inside the castle, however. He had to be summoned, at the very least implicitly.

What had *happened*?

His new bearer's expression had shifted. She eyed him much as she would a wild animal, one quiescent for the moment but otherwise of uncertain temper. "Okay. Look, go sit down or something. We'll have burritos, and then I have some errands to run." Her pupils changed slightly, and he could smell the lie. She was increasingly nervous.

Hal lifted one hand, as if swearing one of Cavanaugh's ridiculous oaths. "You do not have to fear me."

"I don't." A wide bright smile, but her grip changed on the glass. Did she think he intended violence? This was extremely interesting.

So, she did not know what she had done. He was required to show her. The terms of the curse were stringent; he could not let a bearer languish in ignorance once he was summoned.

"The ring you wear is powerful. It was crafted in the great age of—"

"Look, that's really fascinating. Come on and tell me more." She brushed past him, down the hall. "Let's see what the weather's like, huh?"

"Weather? My lady, you must listen. I am required to explain the—"

"Oh, come on." She reached another door, this one securely locked, and spent a few moments fiddling with the mechanisms. He followed, reluctant but impelled. "Okay, this way." She took his arm, and he was over the threshold in a trice, obeying the tacit pressure of her small hand. "There. That's just great."

He was now in a long hall, with doors on either side, all matching hers. Now it made sense—they lived stacked in boxes. Perhaps she was not as wealthy, or she preferred the closeness to others of her kind. "You must listen, the ring—"

"It's a piece of junk jewelry I picked up for a song. Goodbye." She was quick, and swept the door closed. He stood, hearing her move the locks, and exhaled sharply.

It was *frustrating*. Even Cavanuagh's first commands, uttered in a portentous mishmash of ancient tongues, had not been this irritating.

Hal stepped *through* the door, a brief pleasurable shiver filling him as he noted its flimsy construction. He would have to attend to that. "You are not listening, my mistress."

Whatever he expected, it was not her reaction—a brief scream, and the water-glass flickered through the air. He did not duck—there was no need, the cup stopped in midair at the end of a long trail of water held in stasis, droplets shimmering in the golden light from bulbs overhead. They had harnessed an elemental force to heat their homes, to give them light to read by, to drive away the dark.

He was, really, quite proud of mortals. He had even been

one, so long ago. Now, however, he was *something else*, and that something tried an encouraging smile at the black-clad, barefoot woman who had gone transparent-pale, staring not at him but at the glass suspended in empty space, the water spinning as it retracted all its tentacles and droplets, becoming a perfect liquid globe.

"You may call me Hal," he repeated patiently. "You are the bearer of the ring, and I am your servant as long as that is so."

Her throat worked. She really was quite pale, and he was half afraid she might swoon. Her gaze flickered to the water, to the floating glass, to his face, and back to the water, which floated to the cup's mouth and crawled in as the cup righted itself, still in midair.

"Um," was all she said, in a quiet, hurt little voice.

It was a start.

❧ 13 ❧

FAIRYTALES CLOSED

EMILY HUDDLED ON HER COUCH, HER LEGS PULLED UP AND her head spinning. This was, without a doubt, the worst hangover she'd ever had.

The guy crouched in front of the television, passing his hands *through* it as if he was a ghost. Or as if the TV was. It made her feel woozy. Now she noticed that her bookshelves were a little disarranged—nothing much, but the dust was disturbed and each book was ever-so-slightly repositioned. As if it had been taken down, flipped through, and carefully replaced.

"You paid for the ring, I presume?" His head turned, a beaky profile. His hair was secured not by an elastic band but by a leather thong, tied in an intricate knot.

"Cash money," she heard herself reply. At least her mouth was still working. "Right on the barrelhead."

His sweater still looked damn familiar, but she couldn't figure it out until she looked at her glass Ikea coffee table and saw the open DVD case. Right on the front was the brooding, almost-handsome star of a tawdry tragedy based on one of those tearjerker novels. The guy was in that same blue sweater, the one worn during the scene where he almost drowned saving the heroine. This...thing, this hallucination, was wearing the same boots, too.

I'm dreaming. I have to be. Except if she was, wouldn't realizing that wake her up? And wouldn't this guy look more like Ontario Cowboy than...whoever he looked like? You couldn't see faces in dreams you'd never seen before. It was science.

"I wonder..." He stood, unfolding gracefully, and turned to regard her. "You still look frightened. There is no need to be."

I'll decide that, thanks. Em searched for words. None seemed to apply. She hugged her knees a bit tighter, staring at him. If not a dream, it was a hallucination—there was no doubt about it. Maybe from the liquor, or more likely from this guy slipping her something while she slept. All she had to do was keep him away from her for long enough and the effects would wear off.

"It was easier last time," he said, his dark gaze roving the apartment as if looking for something. "Then, they knew what they were seeing."

This guy's fucking crazy. "So, uh..." Her throat was dry, and her head still wasn't happen even though the aspirin had kicked in. "So what *am* I seeing?"

He spread his arms a little, palms out. Even with his shoulders not quite wide enough, if he hadn't been bugfuck nuts, she could even see glancing at him twice in a bar. He looked serious, just on the edge of homely, but there was a certain something around the mouth that might have almost been worth finding out about.

He had a shadow. The floor made its regular sounds when he stepped from carpet to linoleum and back. Someone peering in through the French door leading to her tiny slice of balcony overlooking the parking lot would think that maybe he was a real person instead of a hallucination. Or that he was a friend of hers, telling her a story that required standing up and pacing to make it coherent.

Something obviously occurred to him, his dark eyes lighting up and his shoulders stiffening a little. Two quick steps took him to the books, where he bent and ran his finger along the second-to-the-bottom shelf. "Ah. This might help."

He dropped the book on the couch next to her, and a snap of his coppery fingers—a crisp, authoritative sound—made it flop open, the pages riffling. She flinched. *Not possible. That's not possible, my God.*

It was the Sunshine Book of Fairy Tales, left over from childhood. She'd rescued it from her mother's great purge of the attic five years ago, maybe on a whim, maybe because the illustrations had once upon a time given child-Em hours of fascination. They were all familiar—Sleeping Beauty, a Rapunzel story where the prince had his eyes clawed out by brambles, Rumpelstiltskin and his big cauldron ready to boil the queen's baby, Jack the Giant-Killer...and Aladdin, whose Princess was swindled by a sorcerer crying *new lamps, new lamps for old!*

He leaned down, apparently not noticing her flinch, and tapped the illustration once. It was the teenage Aladdin in watercolor, his face a mask of fear, rubbing the magic lamp. Swirls of fluorescent glitter zoomed around him, the magic garden deadly as it was beautiful, and that was partly why it had never been her favorite tale.

Poor old Aladdin just looked too damn *scared*.

"Yours is no lamp, but a ring." The guy smiled, kindly enough. This close you could see the corners of his eyes crinkle, and a faint shadow of stubble. Surely no hallucination could be this *detailed?* He retreated, again spreading his hands again as if he was trying to appear harmless. It looked like a habitual movement. "I am your servant, Mistress. In all ways, until you are dead or the ring is taken from you."

"Oh, Jesus," Em whispered. "You are *so nuts*."

Another helpless little gesture. He had a large stock of them, it seemed. "What would it take, for you to believe?"

Em rested her forehead on her knees. "Can I wish I never bought the damn ring?"

"You could. The side effects might be...unpleasant. Time is not to be meddled with lightly."

Her fingers began to crawl over each other. Warm metal, the flat glassy stuff over the slice of agate or whatever it was, the way it fit her finger. It was even comfortable to sleep in, for God's sake, she didn't feel like she'd swelled around it.

She tugged at the setting, at the bottom of the loop, trying to slide it off her finger.

It wouldn't move. She tugged harder and harder, but the ring didn't budge. It wasn't precisely *stuck*, it was just like trying to yank her own skin off.

All of a sudden, his hands closed over hers, and she flinched. His skin was very warm, and very different than hers. Rougher, but his hands felt...human.

Her stomach turned over, and the thought that she was going to vomit water-laced bile all over him was only faintly embarrassing. She could still smell the coffee, with its faint cooked undertone that meant it had been in the pot for a while. Her legs prickled a little; she hadn't shaved since Thursday morning.

He squeezed, gently. "You will harm yourself, Mistress."

"My name is Emily," she whispered.

"And you may call me Hal."

Paul Simon began playing in her head. Not a bad earworm, but it fucking sucked to have the radio in her head turn on when she was struggling to figure out just how long she'd have to wait for the drugs to wear off, for the...

It was like thinking through mud, but she gave it a try. "Can I wish you away?"

His face changed. Em pushed herself backward, her heels digging in, but he just let go of her hands and stood, arms dangling loose at his sides. Even the cabled knit of his sweater was too detailed to be imaginary. "You may return me to my resting-place until you have further need of me."

Well, that sounds promising. There was a rushing noise in her ears, making it difficult to think *or* talk. "How do I do that?"

"Simply dismiss me."

"How do I do *that?* I need details."

His eyebrows—very dark, his hair was like ink, really— drew together. His shoulders lifted a fraction. "Have I somehow displeased you?"

"Look, dude, I don't know what you slipped into my drink, but I don't like it. You can go wherever you like, just leave me alone."

His mouth turned into a thin line. His eyes flashed, and chin set stubbornly. "Is that a command?"

At least he hadn't gotten violent. This was edging over to "hallucination" instead of "drugged-out nutbar," which was a relief. But still. "Sure. You can go do whatever you want, but leave me alone."

She wasn't prepared for the result. There was a tiny *pop* of collapsing air, and the hallucination vanished. A soft breeze, redolent of cardamom, touched her cheek and her tangled hair, riffled the pages of Sunshine Fairy Tales. Em actually started and let out a tiny, undignified squeak. She rubbed her face, peeking through her fingers every few moments as if he would come back. She tugged on the ring again, decided it was probably stuck because she was alcohol-bloated and she could get it off later.

For right now, though, she slowly, cautiously uncurled. Gained her feet, trying to look everywhere at once. She flipped the battered book of fairytales closed, swept it off the couch, and kicked it so it slid underneath. Once it was out of sight, she felt a lot better. She could have imagined the whole damn thing. Everything, from the blue sweater to the tiny sound the pages made when the book opened on its own, all the way to the floating waterglass.

"Never drinking again," she whispered. "Never, ever drinking again."

She marched into her kitchen, and took a long look at the glass on the counter, still full of tapwater. It sat there as if it had never intended to move, as if the morning's fun and games were just that: a momentary blip in an otherwise well-ordered schedule. After a few moments of deep thought, her cheek twitching a little like her mother's when exhaustion or irritation had reached monumental levels, she dumped it out and dropped the glass into the trashcan. She had half-a-dozen more, she could tell herself she'd broken that one and forget the whole episode ever happened. She poured out the cooked coffee, too, but she couldn't afford to put *that* in the trash. She could, however, tell herself she'd set it last night in a fit of drunken preparation and "accidentally" slop a lot of it down the shower drain while she soaped.

That was her plan, and it was a good one.

Now, what did a woman who just dispelled a hallucination do? What was normal and sane?

A shower next, Em decided. Her head throbbed, but after she stood under some hot water she could pretend she'd just gotten up, make some fresh coffee, and order some burritos. She could watch a little TV and just chill, like any normal, healthy-minded woman.

Okay. That was her plan.

She dropped the shampoo bottle twice. Her hands refused to stop shaking.

❧ 14 ❧

NOT OUTRIGHT

CLOAKED AND HOODED IN BLACK, THE MEN GATHERED. A low humming of expectation filled the circular room, and candles in waist-high, branching holders coyly fluttered their flames. Electricity didn't like the sort of work performed down here, and after the first few instances with shattered lightbulbs, the wiring had been removed. The entire affair had been expensive, and there had been trouble afterward, too. The old man didn't understand that you couldn't just make people disappear after they did your remodeling, not when they were licensed and bonded.

Of all the times Peter had seriously considered taking a drastic step, that one had been the second-closest. In retrospect, it was a good thing he'd refrained. It didn't pay to be hasty.

The walls were oak, the ceiling vaulted and painted with squiggles that looked random unless you were initiated. Then, you could see the invisible lines connecting the painted bits, and the illustrations moved slowly between ceremonies. The Bull, the Serpent, the Rat, and the Vulture watched whatever occurred underneath them, and sometimes their expressions were almost...well, almost sentient.

Lines and circles grooved deeply into the marble below Peter's feet, the great double circle and its smaller orbiting symbols subtly vibrating. They could be moved, too, holding the configuration of the last Work performed within them or sliding into place once the ceremony was started. For that reason alone, there needed to be trained anchors in the orbiting symbols.

"Are you *sure*?" Henry Maggs said, again, scratching at his hairline under the hood's capacious shadow. He looked like a waddling friar, mostly because the knot on his velvet-rope belt was sloppy. He was in Nikes, too, instead of ceremonial boots, and his spray tan had deepened.

Peter said nothing. He simply assumed his place inside the circle at the pole—one of the points of the interlocked triangles deeply cast into the smooth concrete flooring.

It was the safest place possible, for once.

"Peter?" Moss piped up, next. "I hate to ask, but—"

The narrow door leading to the stairs opened, its hinges whisper-soft, and everyone froze.

The old man, his robe swaying softly, stepped through. With his hood back, his lank hair scraped back into a pony-tail, and his hazel eyes wide and dancing, he looked like a fellow who felt young again, with a bounce in his step and a song in his black little heart.

Maggs gasped audibly. Grosvenor stiffened, his robe rippling, and Moss shut his mouth so fast the click of his teeth meeting was a good billiards crack.

The bulb on the tip of the old man's nose twitched, once. His strong yellowed teeth showed in a wide smile, the expression of a man contemplating something he had paid for and couldn't wait to use. His old, glove-soft leather boots, custom made a few years ago by a master cobbler in Spain who demanded a tracing of horned, stub-toed feet and a truly staggering fee, were freshly polished. He was, Peter thought, probably naked underneath the yards of soft black cloth.

"Good evening, gentlemen," he said, and minced past a bank of candles as the door quietly, in defiance of all logic and rationality, closed itself.

And locked.

The map, brushed carefully free of broken glass, was stretched on the desk in the study at Peakes End. Its inked lines trembled, and there were spots all over the faithful rendering of the modern city where the interference was too high. In one of those spots, the new owner of the fantastical thing that kept the old man alive was hiding. The thing bound into the ring—and by now, Peter was cautiously believing some of the old man's wilder stories—would no doubt be reflexively cloaking its position now that it was active.

Where there was a will, though, there was a way. The old man had finally calmed down enough to pull a thick tome bound in discolored leather from the shelves and flipped through it, muttering, then told Peter to call the inner circle.

"Good evening, sir." Bruce Vance was quicker off the mark than anyone else. He executed a little half-bow, and the old man beamed pacifically in his direction. Now they could see what he was carrying—a somewhat antique birdcage, its bottom almost rusted through. Inside it, fur quivered and a single dark eye blinked once before the three rats—black, brown, and white—huddled even closer together, as if they sensed what was about to occur.

Vance's small movement may have changed the old man's mind about a critical part of the ceremony. "You, you, and *you*." One spidery pale hand pointed at Moss, Maggs, and Sampson. "Take the inner triangle tonight, and each of you with a chalice. Peter, you will hold the pole. The rest of you, find your places."

They fairly leapt to obey, except Peter, who had arranged himself inside the smaller circle at the pole already. The old man set the cage in the very center of the circle, on the low stone plinth mostly used for charging objects with invisible force. The candleflames flattened, recovered.

Practice made the energy-charge larger. When you carried enough, all sorts of strange things could happen, the world arranging itself around you in patterns like iron filings around a magnet. It took a lot of work to keep the levels up, so to speak, another reason why this sort of thing was left to men of leisure. Only the most naturally gifted of nine-to-five drones could manage even a weak charge.

The old man, of course, had nothing else to do all day but practice. And watch the History Channel, and drink.

Peter quelled the urge to slide his hand through the slit in his robe and touch the cold hilt at his side. All that extra material covered all sorts of bulges, and the hood would shadow his expression. He pulled it up further, settling it against his hair. A small, icy prickling slid down his back.

One of the rats, braver than his cohorts, lifted his narrow pink nose, sniffing distrustfully.

"*Somnis,*" the old man whispered, spreading his left hand over the cage, and the creature subsided, sinking into a slack, furred heap.

"Never been *inside* the circle before." Moss sounded very jolly, his cheeks quivering a little. He hadn't taken off his watch, either. The Rolex gleamed as he spread his hands, his eyebrows coming up. "Ooooooh!" A childish bit of clowning around.

Peter's lips stretched into an approximation of a smile. Though he didn't know it, he looked very much like his great-

great-great grandfather in that moment. The hood dipped lower, keeping him safe.

No, you couldn't make people outright disappear anymore. Not pillars of the community, active in the Sophics or the Masons or the Chamber of fucking Commerce.

Not outright.

But you could drain a modern person past belief, past sanity, and implant a suggestion to have them dispose of themselves. Nice, neat, tidy—and something Peter was very good at. He had already earmarked replacements for after this night's work. It would have to be handled delicately indeed. Which meant Peter's own position was relatively safe.

Until the old man got his hands on this ring.

Oh yes. There were other plans to be made. Peter sank his heels into the marble floor, inhaled deeply, and shook his hands out. Once the chanting started, none of the men inside the middle circle would be able to move. They would be struck dumb, able only to breathe as the work bore down on them.

Beasts to the slaughter. They didn't even suspect.

15
FAR LESS COMFORTABLE

Do what you like. Just stay away from me.

How many times had Hal dreamed of this very independence? He was a bird, wheeling over this great stone-colored city, the spines at its heart higher than even the loftiest cathedral spire, the mortals zooming in their metal chariots or hurrying along damp, chilly streets of paving or poured stone —*concrete*, he reminded himself—that even the Romans in their arrogance might envy. The palaces that had seemed so fabulous last night were now, as he understood, relatively simple homes. The city spread, and sprawled, full of color and vitality, gigantic metal trucks nosing up to its buildings and disgorging every manner of goods, ateliers on every corner, for every conceivable service.

The bounty was not shared equally, even though there was enough and to waste. *The poor are always with you*, the prophets always remarked, for no other reason than it was true. There was a vast underclass clinging to respectability and the large glowing screens they used to numb themselves, and an even lower class of rejects and castaways, immigrants and laborers. Then, there were the beggars, picking at the edges and living wherever they could hide.

For all that, they did not reek as the poor had during his last sojourn here. Cavanaugh's time had not been as foul as, say, Rheims in the time of his fiftieth bearer—or was it the fifty-second? They had changed so frequently in those days.

The Inquisition saw to that.

He could walk alongside them, peering through their fantastical windows at the shapes and colors on display. He could pass unseen, if he wished, plunging through the large buildings and drinking in small doses of their lives, their joys, their fears, their anger. He could summon one of the metal chariots and learn its use and construction. He could plunder their libraries, their museums...

Hal banked sharply, wind ruffling through feathered wings and crested head. This shape was not his favorite, built more for gliding than for actual flight, but until he had studied the local fauna he was forced to be expedient rather than camouflaged. His feet, now equipped with sharp talons, opened and closed as if they felt prey. Why had he turned?

My bearer.

The woman. He was unused to venturing this far from the ring's holder. He was bound to guard the bearer, but her command... What had he expected? They were fragile, irrational creatures. He had not been prepared for skepticism. Weren't females supposed to be more superstitious, less armored against spirits and strong winds? He should have had no trouble dealing with a single unaccompanied girl.

And yet. Had he been a mortal man, he would have been left outside her door, scratching his head and wondering what had just happened. A feat perilously close to magic.

He could go wandering, cramming as many new experiences and concepts into himself as possible, until she met with an accident. The ring would not relinquish her until he had performed at least one work at her direct bidding, and if she took it off after only one, he would be returned to the castle to wait for another of her ilk or Cavanaugh's to free him.

What was this time she lived in, if she could *disbelieve* so thoroughly? Last time he had been so careful not to give himself away, both under Cavanaugh's orders and because many mortals of that time were capable of great violence against those they suspected of trafficking with something outside the Church. His bearers could be injured or even killed by those who knew what they were about and had some patience.

Or an invisible ally of their own.

His feathers melted and he dove, a vivid boiling streak plummeting from a gray sky. He landed on a strip of pavement next to a bridge full of those whizzing cars, his feet now solid and booted, the rest of him a man dressed just as these others did—harsh blue breeches, cotton shirt, woolen sweater, and an overcoat that lacked the flair of a gentleman's cloth. Still, they were warm and comfortable, but something troubled him.

None of the cars veered when he made his appearance. None of them turned to stare. He had dropped out of the sky, and they did not look.

They did not *notice*.

He headed for the south end of the bridge, changed his mind, turned back to pace north. Stopped between steps, shook his dark head, and whisked invisibility over himself with an unnecessary gesture. In all the endless time of his service, he had never felt this...*disconcerted*.

This anonymous.

It was much better than the boredom, but far less comfortable.

"Well," he said aloud, relishing the weight of his voice

even as it was lost under the noise of the rushing chariots. She had not barred him specifically from *watching*, she just said to stay away. There was no specified distance he had to observe. As long as she was not alerted to his presence, he was obeying the command. It wasn't a wonder performed for her, but he could wait. Sooner or later she would speak the fateful words again, and he would be ready.

Hal grinned, his invisible body whirling catlike, and he leapt to the bridge's railing. Looking down upon a dizzying river of metal and concrete, he exhaled sharply and stepped out into empty air. A flash, a burst of black feathers, and he was airborne again, winging toward the unphysical throbbing that was his fetter, clasped on the hand of a mortal girl.

16

A LITTLE TENSE

IT WASN'T WORKING.

There were dishes of "leftover" Halloween candy on every desk—Patty Larogue had brought in bags and bags of it, just like she did every year. Em couldn't even bring herself to peel a mini Snickers bar, let alone open up a butterscotch. Her stomach kept rolling over every time she reached for the sugar, and that was only the beginning of the problems. Coffee gurgled behind her breastbone, even dipping French fries in a chocolate milkshake hadn't been as appetizing as she thought it would, and apparently her favorite bra was developing a rubbing underwire to add to the fun. Her stockings kept slipping, the side zipper on her slacks had frozen four-fifths of the way to the top, and the goddamn spreadsheets were acting like a divine hand had suddenly fucked with both the laws of mathematics *and* the core programming functions.

To top it all off, the ring was still on her finger, its band refusing to let go of her skin. It was comfortable enough, except every time she looked at it, her stomach did another flip.

She pushed back from the desk, pinching the bridge of her nose to stave off the headache already poking at her temples, and her cellphone buzzed. It was a number she didn't recognize, so she just let it run to voicemail and continued massaging where her nose met her eyebrows. At least there wasn't a meeting this afternoon, and Funke wouldn't be asking her for the reports just yet.

"Small mercies," she muttered, and just as her phone stopped buzzing, someone's hands descended on her shoulders.

Emily yelped, leaping to her feet, and the chair rammed back into Brett's legs. He let out an *oof* and the entire fish-bowl went silent. Even the people on calls paused, and Em could almost *feel* the entire office's collective ears perking.

"What are you *doing?*" It burst out before she could stop herself, the words not quite reaching break-a-window shrill only because most of her breath was gone already. "What the hell?"

Brett's face fell, but there was a ratty little gleam of enjoyment in his chilly blue eyes. "Didn't mean to scare ya, honey." Today, the pastel tie was sherbet-orange, but his shirt was the same as ever—blue, white collar and cuffs. No suspenders, but the pleats on his pants were knife-sharp. Maybe he even used spray starch.

Do not call me "honey", you waste. "What do you want, Brett?" Again, she was too loud, and visions of grabbing her stapler and smacking him in his perfect teeth were dancing *really* close to the edge of her impulse control.

He was getting all sorts of reaction from her; his delight was almost palpable. "You just looked a little tense, that's all."

"If I'm *tense* it's because you're always sneaking in here and touching me without my permission." Em realized her hands were shaking, but it wasn't likely to be noticeable because she'd clenched them into fists. "Do you have some work-related reason for coming into my cubicle?"

"Whoa!" He held his hands palm-out, a mocking little grin exposing those magnificent, expensive teeth. He'd gotten some notice, and some interaction. A big dose of each. He was probably in hog heaven. "Just contributing to a friendly workplace culture, that's all. I was heading to the break room, you want some coffee?"

I'll just bet you were. "No, thanks." She tried not to sound sarcastic, and suspected she failed. Her heart pounded so fast she felt lightheaded, and her knees were suspiciously shaky. "Stop coming in here and trying to scare me, Brett."

Paper rustled, and curly-headed, lanky Becky Cornight in the cubicle next to Em's stood up, stretching, wide-eyed and innocent. "Hey Em," she said, salting the first half with an only partly theatrical yawn. "You got a minute?"

"Sure I do." Em stared at Brett, hoping her resting bitch-face was enough to deter him.

Becky cleared her throat, and she glared meaningfully at Brett, too. He just stood there, obviously enjoying the attention.

Jesus. Fucking. Christ. Em's jaw ached, her teeth ground together so hard she could almost hear the stress-groaning. Imagining hair-fine cracks opening up in her molars was not helping either.

Her imagination just worked too goddamn well.

Becky cleared her throat a second time. "Go on your break, Brett. We wouldn't want to keep you."

"Sure you don't want anything?" His blue gaze dropped to Emily's chest. She didn't have a clue *why*, for God's sake, the silk button-down and lovely navy sweater she'd put on this morning were not even close to revealing attire. But apparently that didn't matter to this asshole. He stared for a full five seconds more before grinning again.

"Absolutely sure," Em managed through her tight-clenched teeth, and watched him retreat for the breakroom with his long, prissy strides. A cloud of his drugstore body spray lingered, and Em sagged against her desk, her hip almost dislodging the printer. "Jesus *Christ*," she breathed as soon as he'd turned the corner.

"I know, right?" Becky's unplucked eyebrows huddled closer together, a furry Gordian knot. "He 'accidentally' bumped up against me in the copy room the other day. It was either a pencil or his boner, I couldn't tell which."

A laugh caught itself in Em's throat, turned into an almost-rancid burp. "A harassment suit waiting to happen."

"I'd file, if I didn't need my paycheck." Becky pushed her hair back, the rhinestone barrette at her right temple winking cheerfully. She'd gotten perfect corkscrews instead of Emily's weird lopsided curls; in the great genetic lottery, Em often felt made out of leftovers. It was too bad her mother couldn't have other kids, but if she had, would that have made things better?

Mom hadn't called yet this week. That was a plus.

"I just wish he'd go away." Emily let out a shaky breath—which turned into a gasp halfway through.

The ring on her left middle finger...twitched. A definite *tug*, and it warmed up as well, as if the metal had been sitting in a sunny windowsill and just now touched skin.

Wait, what? What did I just—

"Hello, mistress." A soft cardamom breeze brushed the stale recycled air pumped through the entire warren. And, leaning nonchalantly right at the edge of her cubicle, his elbow resting on the three-quarter wall and his dark hair pulled severely back, the guy from her Halloween hallucination regarded her steadily.

Em's jaw dropped. She glanced at Becky, but Becky wasn't looking at her. Instead, eyes glazed, Becky stared into space, her mouth slightly open, her hand caught in the act of brushing her hair back. She wasn't moving.

She was...frozen. Trapped. Paused like a DVD.

Em's hands flew to her mouth, clapping over a rising scream.

"There is no need to cry out," the hallucination repeated. "You have summoned me, and I am here."

"I did *not*—" she began hotly, even though she was only addressing a fever dream or some neurons misfiring or—

"You did." His smile wasn't as expensive as Brett's, but it was sort of...terrifying. Because it seemed so *genuine*. "But I wish to please you, so I shall ask, do you wish that man erased as if he had never lived? Or do you wish him banished to some remote place where he will slowly starve to death? A desert island, perhaps? Or should I simply unmake him where he stands? If you prefer the last, I suggest you direct me to leave his clothes behind. That will provide all manner of amusement."

Em whirled, shoving her chair into the doorway to block it. She clambered up onto her desk, grabbed the top of the filing cabinet in one corner, and stared out over the office.

There was Delbert Clive, throwing his stupid Koosh ball in the air while on a client call, leaning back in his office chair. The ball hung in midair, and Del had been caught in mid-blink, his mouth open and his tongue on his lower teeth. Peggy Brampton was in the main corridor behind the empty cubicle set against the rear of Em's, caught while scratching at the side of her nose while her ankle buckled slightly, a prelude to a stumble. And there was Patty, at her admin's desk in the very center, her nose less than an inch from her screen, probably typing up a gossipy email about how Em had yelled at Brett.

"I'm insane," Em breathed. "I'm dreaming. I'm hallucinating."

"No," he said, softly, persistently. "You are the ringbearer, and I am your servant. Now, tell me, where *precisely* do you wish to send that man?"

✺ 17 ✺

MIRACLE FULCRUM

SHE CLIMBED DOWN FROM THE FLIMSY DESK WITH admirable grace. Hal's eyelids dropped halfway as she approached him, and he was almost charmed when her right hand, kept low at her hip, struck up and out, the small iron thing whacking him solidly in the stomach. Had he been mortal, it might have discommoded him, but instead she dropped the thing—*stapler*, he found the word for it floating on the air—with a clatter and snatched her hand back with a soft, completely unconscious sound of surprise. It would have been like striking a concrete wall, for her.

It was pleasant to set aside the invisibility, for once. Watching her had taught him much of this strange new modern world, and he found there was much to like about this new mistress. She seemed unruffled by the high speed of their chariots, and occasionally, when she answered the—*telephone*, he reminded himself—sitting on her desk next to the glowing screen her greetings were always soft and pleasant. Her apartment was neat, her furniture well cared for, and the more he watched the more odd he found it that she was not married. Surely she should have suitors?

"I am real enough." He watched expressions flit across her face—large dark eyes outlined with kohl, that lucid mortal skin, the glossy hair half-held back. Had he at first thought her only winsome? In Cavanaugh's day, she would have been the belle of any gathering, and yet here she wore a man's breeches and sat for hours staring at a glowing screen, murmuring to herself and making numbers dance. Hal offered his hand. "Here. Touch me, if it will help you believe."

She shook her head. Her throat moved as she swallowed. "I thought I told you to go away." Her voice gathered strength; she was gaining courage.

"You summoned me."

"I just said I wi—" She actually clapped her right hand over her mouth again, which robbed him of the pleasure of looking at its shape, but it made her eyes much larger. "Oh," she said, muffled into her palm. "*Oh*."

She was intelligent. Almost harmfully so. "Very good. The wish summons your servant. I repeat, which way do you wish him to vanish? You can leave the choice to me, if you like. He seems a foul-mannered man, indeed." Though what a woman could expect parading around in breeches *and* unescorted, Hal could not tell.

"Uh." Her hand dropped back to her side. She visibly struggled with the implications of the question. "Um. Okay. Look, have you stopped time, or..."

"We have only moved very slightly sideways for a moment. Still, I advise you not to delay your decision overmuch." The complexity of the operation he had performed would be, he suspected, largely lost on her. Most of his bearers had not wanted to know the how, only the possible fulfillment.

"Okay." His bearer nodded. She was altogether too pale. "Okay. I'm asleep at my desk, and this is a really vivid dream. So, let me ask, how many wishes do I get? Three?"

None of the others had thought him a dream. "As many as you like, while wearing the ring."

"How long do I get to wear the ring?"

Another good question. Very practical, this woman. Almost *too* practical. "As long as you like."

"And if I take it off?" A faint note of challenge, eyes narrowing slightly and head tilting, her arms coming up to cross defensively over her chest. Her shirt and sweater blurred her outline, but only pleasantly so.

"You've already tried." It wasn't quite an answer, but Hal suspected the finer points would be lost on her in the current situation. And, strangely, he did not wish for this particular bearer to slip the ring free just yet. "While you are the bearer I may not harm you, allow you to come to harm, or cause you harm by inaction."

That got a response—a small, coughing, disbelieving laugh. "Man, I definitely read too much Asimov in college."

"Azee—" He was about to ask, but she shook her head again, her curls swaying heavily.

"Not important. Okay, so this is a dream. Right. Fantastic. Good. Can you send Brett somewhere else? Some other job with comparable pay and benefits, where...where he isn't able to harass women ever again? Can you do that?"

"If you wish it so." *Harass? What an odd term.* And a tender-hearted request, too. "Do you?"

"Yeah. Sure. And then you can, I don't know, go help a little old lady across a street or something like a good little magical Boy Scout."

"Is that a command?"

Her eyes could not become any wider. "Um, no. I'm not big on the commanding thing."

"That is a great pity." He waited, but she just stood there, staring at him. Was he exotic to her, as well? He had never considered a bearer's...feelings?—before. Then again, they had known what they were summoning. "May I, my mistress?"

"Gonna go home and watch some *Dream of Jeannie* reruns," she muttered. "Yes, sure. Knock yourself out."

So. His first true act for this new bearer, then. He concentrated upon the parameters set by her stipulations, and it could have been that easy. However, he had learned long ago that they needed a few...theatrics.

Hal lifted his left hand and snapped, twice. The sounds crackled, there was an echoing *crack* of the sideways-turning thread drawn back into the regular stream of time, a brief sliding sensation as the stream absorbed and righted the molecule-thin rivulet. There was a brief hissing, and Hal stepped aside through folded space, resolving into visible corporality to watch as the man Brett, who had stealthily crept upon Hal's bearer with lust written across his features, tumbled naked down a sandy, thorn-clad slope. At the bottom was a tangle of giant metal tubes and spurting fire, black smoke rising from one tall tower, and the place was a filthy blot upon the landscape. In the distance, mountains rose their great unconcerned heads topped with white, and Hal longed to visit them.

The urge to return to his bearer was almost as strong, for once.

The vast complex was an oil refinery, and the man Brett now was employed there with a comparable rate of pay and benefits. There were very few women within fifty miles, the ones working at this place would be almost invisible to Brett, and as an additional fillip, the next time a woman was uncomfortable in Brett's presence for any reason, the uncouth beast would begin to vomit uncontrollably.

It struck Hal as fitting. He snapped again, and the man was suddenly in dungarees and a rough cotton shirt, heavy boots caked with wet dirt and undergarments as uncomfortable as Hal could make them.

He watched as the man picked himself up at the bottom of the slope and shook his blond head, dirt and sand vengefully sliding into every small crevice of flesh or cloth it could find. Soon the whistle would blow, and it would be time to return to work, and the man's bafflement would be complete.

She had not specified that Brett would *keep* the job, after all.

The effect began at Hal's toes and rose, a slow wave of pleasure. Performing a work rewarded him. He had long fought it, thinking it would make him slavish, but really, why should he not enjoy what he did? Cruel or compassionate, his bearers were helpless without him. He was the fulcrum that moved miracles through the world, and this small recompense was only his due.

He wrapped invisibility around him again, but when he returned to his bearer's small office by taking another small sideways step, she was not there.

❧ 18 ❧

THE GUYS IN THE WHITE COATS

HER PHONE BUZZED AGAIN JUST AS HER CAR STARTED. SHE grabbed it and her thumb hit the *accept* instead of *decline*. "*Shit*," she almost-yelled, and decided maybe it was May. The laurel hedge in front of her usual parking spot sparkled with rain as the clouds parted enough to let a single lone sunbeam through. There were going to be rainbows.

And she was not dreaming. Or if she was, it was a particularly vivid nightmare.

"Nope, just me," the caller said. His voice sounded oddly familiar. "Is this Emily? Emily Maldean?"

He even pronounced it right. Em grabbed her scattered wits, buckled her seatbelt, and dropped the car into reverse. "Do I owe you money?"

"Nope. This is Jake, from the Halloween party. Your friend May gave me your number, and I thought I'd call rather than text, because it's less—"

"Who?" She backed out in a hurry, saved from hitting another car by the fact that nobody had parked next to her. The firm was renting this huge suburban office space from an even bigger company, but they only occupied about a third of it. "I'm sorry, but *who?*"

Brett's red Toyota had been in the next row when she arrived that morning. She'd noticed it because he'd taken up two spaces, as usual, as if a Corolla could ever have that valuable a paint job.

It was gone. The two empty spaces were like knocked-out teeth, staring at her.

"The cowboy from Ontario. Listen, I wanted to make sure you got home all right, and—"

What. The fuck. "May gave you my number?" This was the absolute last thing she needed.

"She did. I also wanted to—" He took a deep breath, and Em stared at the gearshift. "I wanted to see if you, um. If I could meet you for coffee somewhere."

Drive. She had to put it into drive if she wanted the car to go forward. "What?" *I am not tracking like I should be.* "Listen, now's not a good time. I'm driving. Thanks for making sure I got home safe. You were a real prince, I'm glad to have met you, and say goodnight, Gracie."

"Goodnight, Gra—"

Well, at least he was fast on his verbal feet. She hit the disconnect, dropped her phone into her purse in the passenger seat, and almost stomped the gas before she realized the car was still in reverse.

Em very carefully pressed the tab, worked the shift lever down to the D, and heard her own breathing, high and sharp. She was making a small wheezing noise, and her vision was doing funny things, narrowing as if she was in a tunnel. She was in no condition to be driving.

She could probably ask her phone for the directions to the nearest mental hospital, except didn't wondering if you were crazy make you halfway sane? Sweat had gathered under her arms and at the small of her back, her bra poked her again, and her heart was pounding like it meant to escape or give her some sort of attack.

Her car eased forward. She made this drive damn near every day, it wasn't even lunchtime, traffic would be minimal. She'd probably get pulled over halfway home. Could genies fix traffic tickets?

The worst part wasn't Becky just staring at her over the wall, then shaking her head and saying *I forgot what I was gonna say. Crazy, huh?* It wasn't even the way Em's heart was pounding so hard she was going to pass out if it kept up, or the fact that there didn't seem to be enough air.

The worst was that Em had edged down the hall to the breakroom and seen, on the floor in front of the violently yellow counter the coffeemaker rested on, a pile of crumpled clothing. Slacks, blue button-down with white collar and cuffs, wingtips, and apparently Brett had been a tighty-whities man.

Which explained a lot, but still. The kicker of it all was the Creamsicle-orange tie, still neatly knotted, a little, empty noose.

Her hands clutched the steering wheel, white-knuckled. She'd told him to go help a little old lady across the street. Was he off doing that?

Christ, she was thinking as if it was *real*. But...that pile of clothes. She should have stuck around to see if anyone else could see it.

Dream. This is a dream. If I really want it to, the car will fly home. I'll wake up now. I really would like to wake up now.

Em set her jaw. She was going to catch hell for just leaving in the middle of the day. She stared out the windshield, checked the gearshift.

"Okay," she told herself. "You're in drive. You're going to drive home. You're going to walk upstairs and shut the door and go take a bath and go to bed. Or call May." The thought of that phone call made a short, acidic chuckle burble in her throat. "Hi, May? Look, I need some help. I'm having hallucinations, can you send the guys in the white coats over? Also, I think someone vanished at work today but left all his clothes behind and..."

Her blue, used, very-good-gas-mileage Honda crept forward, rolling to a stop at the end of the row. She checked both ways as if traffic might be coming, cut the wheel and risked going a little faster. She could focus on one intersection at a time.

The sun peeked out again as she turned onto 168th. The commute was pretty awful, but her job wasn't bad. She was probably going to get fired for running out in the middle of the day. Then she would probably starve, ending up homeless in an alley shaking a tin can and raving about genies. They weren't kidding when they said drinking could ruin your life.

She hit the freeway southbound with no snags, and with each humming mile her breathing evened out and the dark clouds at the corners of her vision faded. Her heart was still going too fast, she was sweating all over and her bra was going to drive her mad, and the ring was glittering on her third left finger but she didn't dare take her hands from the wheel.

The exits ticked off, one by one. Hers was coming up, and she let out a half-sob, half-laugh of sheer gratitude.

That was when a soft warm breeze caressed her cheek, carrying with it a thread of cardamom. There was a dark bulk in the passenger seat that hadn't been there a moment ago.

"Where are we going?" he inquired, mildly.

Em screamed, the wheel jerked, rubber screeched, and they were airborne.

A JOLT. A BRIEF SECOND OF BLACKNESS STARRED WITH HARD cold points of light. Her scream dissolved into a wrenching gasp, and she leaned over, retching. There was an iron bar across her stomach—his arm, and he just stood there, holding her as if she weighed nothing.

She heaved, but nothing came out. It occurred to her that she was staring at her very own kitchen floor, with its tiny pebble-tiles, hard to scrub and even worse to kneel on to look for something. A dreamy, disconnected desire to not throw up on a nice clean floor managed to back everything down her throat, bile burning as it retreated. She hung there, limp with relief for a few moments, until the thought that she was in shock or dead, trapped in the tangled wreckage of her nice little blue Honda, brought her back with a jolt and she jerked, trying to get away from his grasp.

He was saying something, over and over, softly. "All is well, mistress. Shh, calm, all is well."

Maybe she'd stumbled out into traffic the night of Gloria's party and this was hell. No, hell wouldn't have hot showers or coffee. Purgatory, then? She could believe in that, but genies were a step too far, as May would say.

Jesus Christ, what would May say about this?

She straightened, and his grip changed. Em put her hands flat against his very broad chest and pushed, but he didn't let go. So she had to look up, and up—he was too *tall*—and into a pair of dark eyes with gold-threaded irises. *Human* eyes, humanly concerned. His mouth was drawn tight, a vertical line just beginning between his arched eyebrows. Even the faint shadow of stubble on his cheeks was there, even his *pores*, and there was no way Em could ever in a million years dream up anything this detailed.

He still didn't let go of her. Yep, built just like a man, and she could even see the small knitted bumps in his sweater's shoulder, a tiny glint of gold at his right ear—a small hoop, because a genie had to have an earring, right? Had he gotten that out of the Sunshine Fairy Tales book?

No, the genie in there had a goatee and weird grayish-green skin. This guy just looked...human.

"My car," Em whispered. His gaze had fastened on her mouth, and that was weird. It should have made her uncomfortable. She should have been screaming and wriggling away. She should have been clawing his eyes out and throwing anything she could reach at him.

Well, in a second or two, I just might. She needed a moment.

"Safely below, where you usually leave it. Would you like to see?" One eyebrow lifted slightly when she began to frantically shake her head. "Easy, mistress. The first time is the hardest."

"My *name* is Emily," she managed, blankly.

"Emily." Was that a smile, tilting up the corners of his lips? The division between lip and skin was a hair-thin line, chiseled to a sharp edge.

No hallucination was this good. "Let go of me."

"Is that a command?"

Every time a woman says that, it damn well is. "Yes."

"Very well." His arm loosened, and hey presto, she was free.

Her hip hit a drawer-pull and her head almost clipped the cabinet door she'd left open this morning to grab her travel cup. Her shoulders smacked into the wall at the end of the kitchen, her Japanese wood-carving calendar swinging slightly and her feet still going, trying to push her back through paint, drywall, lumber, and anything else in her way. Her silver garbage can was knocked aside and waltzed up against the fridge with a cheery *bong* sound that would have been hilarious if it had happened at any other time.

His hands fell back to his sides. Em's were fists. Her throat was a desert, and she was dizzy. "I would have died." *I sound like I'm about to scream.*

"Perhaps. But I was there."

Well now, wasn't that the whole problem? Em set her shoulders, wishing she had May's talent for just going with the bizarre no matter how deep it got. "Okay." She folded her arms, tried to peel herself away from the wall. Tried again, and this time, succeeded. "You, uh..."

What would May do?

Well, when she put it that way, sangfroid was just within the range of options. "You—do you want some coffee?"

19

UNINTENDED
CONSEQUENCES

WHATEVER RESPONSE HE HAD EXPECTED, IT WAS NOT THIS brittle calm.

"It's not espresso," she said, measuring out something that smelled very familiar. Coffee. A whole bag of the beans, an utter luxury, and she even had a small whirring contraption to grind them. "I've had my eye on a sweet little Breville machine for a while, but it's a bit steep, you know? So I just have this Mr. Coffee but the beans are fresh." Her hands shook, and her voice was a little too high, but all in all, she was...remarkably...

Hal couldn't find the word. He was sure there was one, but it escaped him at the moment.

"The really important thing is to—look, can you say something? Anything? I'm really trying here." A dark curl fell in her face, she shook it away with a nervous toss of her fine head.

Just like a beautiful, skittish thoroughbred. One that needed a gentle hand, a soothing voice, and absolute trust in her rider. One that did not suffer fools gladly, if at all. "It is a difficult thing." His throat was dry. "You are doing...very well."

"Gee, thanks." Sarcasm, and another toss of those long curls, working their way free of the pins and small elastics holding them back. "It's not every day a Halloween genie crashes my car. So, uh, what did you do to Brett? Please tell me you didn't kill him."

"You specified a different job, comparable pay and benefits, somewhere he could not make women uncomfortable. Not death."

"That's comforting. So what *exactly* did you do?"

"He is employed at an oil refinery." Hal weighed whether or not to tell her the rest. He could not *lie*, but he did not have to—

"Well, that will work off some of his pudge," she muttered. She flicked a switch and the machine gurgled into life. "Shit!" She picked up a forgotten part of it—the basket holding a paper filter and the ground beans, very cleverly constructed—and shoved it home with surprising force. "So, uh, can I unwish things?"

"Do you want to?" He sniffed cautiously. Yes, it was good coffee—*potio Arabica*, Cavanaugh had called it when in the mood for a witticism. Hal had already decided he liked *this* bearer far more than the last. At least she was interesting. Far easier on the eyes. And much, much gentler. Cavanaugh's tastes ran to vengeance, noxious mischief—and flaying the skin from those who displeased him heartily enough.

She examined the coffee machine critically as it began to burble. Her breeches were soft, and though the bottoms were cut for boots, the top showed more of her fine hips than had ever been permissible in Cavanaugh's time. "Well, he's a creep. But it's not exactly fair of me to just...you know, *wish* him away. It's not ethical."

Hal shrugged. Cavanaugh—and indeed, most of his

bearers—had not worried overmuch about such things. "It is as you wish it, mistr—ah, Emily."

A steady amber stream plashed down into the waiting glass pot. She kept stealing nervous little glances at him, those wide dark eyes—there was moss in their depths, like a still quiet pond, hints of dark green in her irises, and now he had been close enough to tell—showing a little white, again like a restive animal's. "You gonna vanish again while you..."

"It is not necessary. I think I'd best stay at your side for a short while." He held himself very still and carefully upright to avoid frightening her further. "You seem...distracted."

"Fucking out of my mind is what I am." Another mutter, this time directed at the sink. She flicked at one of the taps, a quick habitual motion, and laved her expressive fingers.

Her language was extraordinary for a woman. Did they all speak thus, now? "I assure you, you are quite sane." *As such things go.*

"My hallucination tells me I'm quite sane." Now she tipped her head back, addressing the ceiling and the marvelous golden light coming from the overhead fixture. "Peachy. Listen...what's your name, anyway?"

I doubt you could pronounce it, even if I could tell you. "You may call me Hal."

"That's great." She finally looked directly at him, not quite meeting his gaze. "But, really, do you have a real name?"

Was she staring at his nose? Did she find it unpleasing? He had not had time to discern which alterations to his appearance would make him acceptable. "I..." How to explain? "It was...lost, Mistress Emily."

"Lost?"

"The...process whereby I became what I am took certain things from me. That was one of them."

"Jesus." Her expression changed from moment to moment. Now it had settled on...what? "You were made?"

The gurgling and sputtering of the coffeemaker underlaid her words. The resultant brew smelled slightly burnt, but otherwise quite palatable.

"Once I was...as you are." He sought the right words, the most careful way of stating it. "A group of men—sorcerers, you might call them—wished to experiment. For whatever reason, I was ideal."

"For whatever reason?" Her shoulders were easing, little by little. "Do you remember...it, do you remember anything else?"

"It was a long time ago." Would she ask how long? None of the others had. His first few bearers had known, but those later did not care. You did not ask a hammer, a wheel, a stylus how old it was. It was simply a tool, one to be used until it was no longer necessary.

"So...like a curse?" Now she leaned forward a little, as if she was staring at the dancing numbers on the glowing screen, trapped in that ill-smelling warren where she spent her days. There was something about her face, though. He couldn't quite place it. Some word he could not draw to the surface of his consciousness.

"Not precisely." The conversation was not going as he had anticipated. He finally found the word he wanted to describe the emotion on her transparent little face, and it irked him.

It was *pity*.

A long moment of silence, during which they studied each other carefully. The coffeemaker continued to burble and exhale. Imagine, women drinking *coffee*. In the privacy of their own rooms, certainly, but still.

"If I take the ring off, what happens to you?"

"You have already tried taking it off." He made the words as neutral as possible. Now was not the moment to ask himself why he was stating it so cautiously. "You may dismiss me, that will return me to my place of waiting."

"Is it...do you like it there? Is it comfortable?" Her shoulders hunched a little. Her sweater was a bit askew, but she made no move to straighten it. She kept nervously shifting her weight from one foot to the other, and he took care to remain immobile, or, if he must move, to do so very slowly.

No bearer had ever asked him *that* question before, either. "It is adequate. I do not..." He was about to say he did not *enjoy* it, but what was that to her? To anyone?

"You don't like it, though." She nodded, slowly. "Jesus. Okay. So...what happens if the ring is...destroyed? Would that work?"

"What?" It was his turn to look shocked, and a quite unfamiliar cold creeping sensation shot up his back. "No. Absolutely not."

The words rang against the cabinets, and the coffeemaker sputtered.

When her eyes were a little less round, and she had swallowed a few times, she continued her questioning. "Why not?"

"The ring's destruction is my death." Formlessness, the void, dissolution. He was not quite ready for *that*.

"Are you sure?" Did she look hopeful? A new light had kindled in those dark eyes, and Hal found himself uncomfortably wondering what else this bearer would ask him. "What if I wished you free? How about that?"

Hal stared at her, his mouth threatening to drop open with sheer disbelief. "I...do not know."

"Should we try it?" It *was* hope, he decided, and it made her brighter. Almost incandescent. Those eyes lit with a deep glow, her entire face changing, color creeping back into her cheeks.

Hal's palms did not sweat like a mortal man's, but it was uncomfortably close. "No, my mistress. It is too great a risk."

He teetered on the edge of saying more, but she turned

abruptly away, her hip striking the edge of the counter. She winced a little, rubbing at it as her other hand lifted with sweet natural grace to open a cabinet. "Okay, well, we can revisit that. Sugar? Or milk? You look like a black coffee kind of guy, but I'm a bad guesser."

Hal's mouth closed with a snap. Of all the people to possess his fetter, how had fate chosen her?

And why, in the name of every god past and present, did the prospect of her wishing his freedom into existence terrify him?

EVENING GATHERED STRENGTH OUTSIDE HER SMALL apartment. His mistress had removed her uncomfortable-looking shoes, pulled her knees up and hugged them, regarding him with large, dark eyes. She seemed much easier now, especially since she had looked down from her bedroom window and seen her metal chariot in its accustomed place, safe and sound. "I'm gonna get fired," she'd muttered, then shook her head and turned away, shooing him toward the living room and the couch with little gestures. She was handling this *remarkably* well. Her hair had come down, and she kept brushing it away with small irritable movements.

Now she sat on the couch, regarding him. "So...just to be sure I have this all straight. All I have to do is say *I wish*—"

"Or let your desire be made known," he added, perched on the other side of the couch, as far away from her as he could manage.

She grew...nervous...if he drew too closely.

"Or tell you I want something, or *command* it, right? And you have to do it."

"If it is within my power, it is done."

"And your power's pretty large."

It almost nettled him. "What would be the point, otherwise? I am no petty spirit, handing out three droplets at a time."

"Okay." Her coffee had grown cold; she lifted the mug to her lips, grimaced a little, and lowered it.

"Allow me?" He leaned closer, slowly, and pointed at the cup. Steam rose in florid curls, and her eyes grew very round again. "Is that better?"

"Pretty handy. You've got a career in foodservice." She uncurled long enough to set the warmed coffee on the table, gingerly, as if she was afraid it might turn into something else, or suspected poison. "So what do I do now?"

None of the bearers had ever asked him *that*. "Whatever you like."

"I mean, like, what can I do? Can I wish for world peace?" She brightened a little. Had he ever had a bearer so expressive?

He almost felt churlish. "That would be difficult. It might have unintended consequences."

"Like what?"

How to explain? "Define *peace*."

"No war."

"Then, the wish might simply remove humanity. No people, no warfare." The shortest solution, and it had almost an elegance to it.

"Wait, you'd do that?" Her nose wrinkled, her lip drew up, and the shocked disgust was almost palpable.

Why should that single little lip-curl trouble him? He hurried to explain. "You must be...careful, of the terms and strictures you apply to your expressed desires. Besides, I am for *your* service, not the tending of crowds." Most of his bearers had comprehended as much. Admittedly, none of them had even considered "world peace" as an option. None of them had been women, either. Perhaps that was it.

"Oh." She considered this, thoughts moving behind those dark eyes.

Hal's discomfort mounted. For a few moments he thought it was a result of her silence, and wondered at it. Then it sharpened, in a familiar unphysical direction. Strange. He had not felt this since...

"Jesus," she whispered, finally. "I can't believe nobody was stupid enough to wish for that and wipe out humanity. Or maybe they did, then they changed their minds? Would anyone even notice? A person could go absolutely crazy thinking about this sort of stuff, you know. Did it happen before? Do you know?"

She expected an answer. Or several of them, in a logical chain.

"No." Hal's attention turned outward, seeking the source of the disturbance. Danger, yes, but from which quarter? Another bearer would recognize his sudden stillness, suspecting unpleasantness but hopefully confident in Hal's ability to turn it aside.

"You don't even *know?*"

Hal rose. Slowly, so she would not be frightened. The large glass door leading out to a thin strip of a balcony was darkening swiftly with dusk's indigo; he paced toward it, his knee brushing her toes as he passed. A different, far more subtle thrill moved through him and he paused, seeking to shelve that distraction and focus on the—

A crash, a glitter of falling glass, and the lean gray hungry form of a creature from nightmares lunged for his mistress, his ringbearer. Who had little time to scream before Hal *moved*, meeting it halfway with a shattering sound, and every light in the apartment died.

❧ 20 ❧

UNDO WHATEVER YOU DID

It was long and quick and hairy, and it moved in a blur. Yellowed teeth snapped as it snarled, and the genie—Hal —had it by the throat. Em scrabbled back along the couch, her palms and heels burning along the fabric; she hit the arm and toppled over it onto the floor, barking her shoulder a good one and barely aware of the noise she was making until she had to whoop in a long lungstarved breath. Another hideous crunching jolt, and a howl that didn't sound like anything, human or otherwise, that should exist outside a horror movie.

Well, she was in one now, wasn't she. A really, really bad one.

Something thudded in her bedroom, and the noise was coming from everywhere, it was hard to think, she scrambled for the door, impelled only by the blind desire to escape, get *away*.

"*Stop!*" Something flew past her, landed with a wet splatting thump. It cut Em's scream in half and she gained her feet with a violent effort, her palms burning and the short hall to the door suddenly funhouse-skewed because she was listing drunkenly, going so fast she could barely stay upright. Her kitchen was a dark hole to her right, she heard something break again and a sliver popped out of her front door. A long pale sword of glued sawdust masquerading as wood, she'd never thought of how *flimsy* the doors were here and she found herself backpedaling, her feet shooting out from underneath her, her ass hitting the hall floor. She could only make a small hurt sound instead of a scream because *something* hit the door again.

It burst inward, a shower of splinters and sawdust and the peephole glittering as it spun, hanging in midair for one long, adrenaline-soaked, nightmarish moment. Amid the rubble was a long gray hairy shape, snuffling through two huge raw wet dishes on its concave face, its eyes tiny blind rolling marbles. It had *claws,* wicked outstretched obsidian scythes, and it hung in the air over her. A long stream of crimson-tinged slaver flew back along its plump cheek, and Em knew, with sick certainty, that it was going to fall on her.

Except it didn't. A blurring streak zoomed from behind her, hit the thing dead-on, and threw it back into the hallway, taking out what was left of the shattered door and a chunk of wall on either side. Em took the only avenue of escape left, rolling sideways, her hair suddenly full of splinters and dust, her eyes smarting, and the...that *thing*, the vision of that *thing* burned into her brain. Its shoulders, the wiry roughness of its pelt, and worst of all, the fact that rags of what had to be Nikes had clung to its broad, clawed feet.

Rags and tatters of human clothing, and a golden gleam at its wrist—a watch?

She banged into the bathroom door, fish-lurched her way over the threshold on her side, and kicked the door shut behind her. Instant darkness, which was worse than she'd expected, enfolded her. She hit her head on the sink's counter as she struggled upright, fumbling at the doorknob to lock it.

Silence, broken only by her panting breath and her finger-nails scratching as she clawed for the light switch, flipped it.

Nothing happened.

A heavy weight of blackness against her eyes, broken only by a thin line of uneven gray at the bottom of the door. Something was breathing inside her apartment, too. Big, chuffing inhales and short explosive exhales, just like a dog.

Sniffing. Something *sniffing*.

She'd never understood the heavy breathing in horror movies before. Now she did. Her own starved, heaving lungs weren't listening to her, and she could hear each tortured gasp, magnified by the tile floor and the mirror and every other hard surface. Singing in the shower sounded good because the acoustics were so great, but now those acoustics were probably broadcasting every sound she made to every corner of the entire building and oh *God,* she was never going to get her damage deposit back, never.

"No." Hal sounded contemptuous. It was a big booming word, and it rattled the darkness around Emily, who shut her eyes, clinging to the doorknob for dear life. "My bearer did not call for thee."

If she kept her eyes closed, she could pretend it wasn't so dark in here, and that—

Another round of snapping, crunching, tearing, awful noises. Em sobbed once, pointlessly, and tried to think of how she was going to escape when she had stupidly locked herself into a dead end.

Sudden silence, the noise cut off cleanly as if with a knife. Em took the deepest breath she could, and held it, straining her ears.

A soft soughing. The smell of cardamom, again. Some-thing bumped her—warm, and living.

Emily yelped and thrashed, kicking and hitting wildly, but it was only the genie. The light overhead took that opportunity to flick back on, and Em saw him right before she whapped him a good one in the eye with her elbow. His head snapped back, he let out a surprised sound, and Em broke the bathroom door off its hinges as she stumbled away.

HER APARTMENT WAS SHATTERED. EMILY STAGGERED TO A halt and turned in a complete circle, her hands flying to her mouth. Her television screen had a hole in it the size of a fist, the French door was in shards, the couch was ripped to hell. Stuffing flew, an out-of-season snowstorm.

Oh Jesus. Oh Jesus Christ. Oh, my God.

Nope. Definitely never getting her deposit back on this sonuvabitch.

Her framed Rossetti print next to the bookcase was smashed and torn. Her bedroom was mostly okay, but something had run into the counter between her kitchen and her minuscule dining room, and from the look of it, had kept on going until it hit the kitchen sink. Her refrigerator listed alarmingly, water was spraying, and her stove had been torn away and was spitting cascades of sparks. Her DVDs were smashed, her bookcase gone, her coffee table—a moving-in present from May—reduced to splinters and shards.

Her hands dropped. She found herself cupping her elbows in her palms, hugging herself so hard her ribs creaked, and turning in another circle. It reminded her of coverage on CNN after a tornado went through a Midwest town. *There's just nothin',* a heavyset dark-haired woman had said, spreading her hands. *What there is, is just torn up.*

The genie stepped out of the bathroom. A chill, raw, autumn wind poured through the broken French door. His eyes sparked for a moment, the light reflecting oddly, and

Emily's hands turned into fists. The ring was still on her left hand, the band warming as it pressed into her palm, and maybe he saw the change in her expression because he was suddenly in front of her as she found herself tearing at her left hand, trying to get her nails underneath the ring to scrape it free.

"No." His own fingers, hard and warm, locked around her wrists. He wrenched her hands apart. "If you take the fetter off, *you are dead*. No, my mistress. No."

She considered screaming. Nothing else had done a whole lot of good so far, and it was awful tempting.

"Listen. *Listen* to me." He yanked on her arms, or maybe she had tried to get away, she couldn't tell. His teeth and eyes glinted, and the stove spat another bright fan of white-hot sparks. "I can repair all this. Tell me to repair it. *Command* me."

Oh, boy. Hallucinations and commands. At least there was no way she could have done all this on her own, right? So either there was a disaster so huge she had lost her mind, or there was a genie in front of her, a real chunk of heavy magical manflesh, who had just had some sort of brawl that reduced her furniture to flinders.

"I don't want this," she whispered. Her throat had been reduced to a pinhole; even if she wanted to scream, she couldn't. There were sirens in the distance. "This is *insane*."

"I know." He took in a sharp breath as if she'd yelled at him. "I am...sorry. Do you wish me to repair your home?"

"Fine." She shut her eyes tightly. "Go ahead. Do it."

But it won't be the same, she told herself. Nothing will.

"Undo it," she whispered. "Undo *everything*."

Did he pause? "If that is your wish," he said, finally, very softly. The sirens stopped, and a soft slithering silence fell. Everything whirled, even though she couldn't see it, and the vertigo was so bad she almost fell over, except for his grip on her wrists. His hands gentled, and he tried to pull her forward, but she remained straight and slim as a sword while stealthy, unholy energy crackle-crept around her crushed and broken life.

21

THE EASIEST WAY

SHE DID NOT SCREAM AGAIN, OR WEEP, OR FLY AT HIM IN A rage. She simply opened her eyes, glanced over the apartment —everything as it had been before the Appetites had arrived, with their obsidian claws and their unerring concave noses— and shook away his hands. Two nervous, delicate steps away, a doe picking her way into an empty meadow. Her chin leveled, and she regarded him steadily.

The silence was intolerable. He bore it, watching her face for any hint of her next command. What would she ask of him now? To *repair* was not to *undo*, but he was given leeway to choose. He did not even need the theatrics when she had her eyes closed.

Still no word. She simply *stared*, and there was a strange glassy quality to her gaze he was not sure he liked.

Outside, the night was quiet. There were no wailing vehicles drawing nearer, clustering the site of an emergency—now *those* were an innovation. An everyday human magic, one so simple and practical even the ones who made him might have approved. For a moment, Hal tried to remember their faces, those rich-robed masters standing in a circle and chanting while his shivering mortal body stung from shallow cuts, blood and sand mixing, a paste of hideous effectiveness.

But that was not a pleasant thought. Instead, he kept studying her face, waiting.

It was odd—her skin was so fine, and her lashes were soft charcoal arcs. There was dust in her hair, and that was not right. Her shirt was torn, and the knee of her breeches. A pale knee showed, with welling ruby droplets. A scratch, merely a scratch, and yet it pained him.

His mouth opened, with no direction on his part. "There are others of your kind who know...the possibilities."

"Possibilities." It was a colorless whisper. Her lips were very pale, and that bothered him. "You mean, *magic*."

Hal almost winced at the word. Still, it was appropriate. "Yes."

"If I..." Her right hand twitched. "If I give them the ring, will they leave me alone?"

"Even if you could remove it, I would not counsel such a thing." Hal weighed the words very carefully. His attention settled on her left hand. If she moved to take the ring off...

No. Do not let her.

What a strange thought. As if he cared who held his fetter. But the arrival of the Appetites had somewhat changed things. Such things were costly to make, requiring much of the vital force drawn from a living human body.

Was Cavanaugh still alive? If he was, how had the ring left his possession? Perhaps others of the Fratres, but why would they let it be lost? The man had sent him away in the midst of a night of drunken wenching, for once not wishing to force Hal to share his debauch. The miracle was that nobody had thought to utter the summoning words while they wore his fetter—or perhaps nobody had thought it looked worth wearing? Or had it sat in a jewel-box, a dusty closet, for a mortal lifetime or two?

He could have spent an eternity in the castle, staring out at the blank gray wasteland outside, powerless to escape. It was unpleasant to contemplate.

Very unpleasant.

"Will they leave me alone?" she repeated. "If I give it to them? *Will* they?"

"It is far more likely you would meet death soon after you handed it over, even if you could take it off." The Fratres would no doubt swiftly put to death anyone not inducted into their fellowship who had discovered such an artifact; if she thought it was impossible to remove the ring and did not send him back to the castle, he could protect her from whatever *else* they would send to collect it.

It was not a *lie*, he told himself. It *was* impossible for her to remove his fetter.

Because he would not allow it.

Her gaze finally dropped. She held her hands out, and her slim fingers shook. The ring looked too large, too barbaric for such soft perfection. One of her nails had torn all the way down to the quick, and another ruby of bright blood welled.

"Jesus," she whispered. "How did anyone else take this thing off?"

I will not tell you. "Some died eventually of old age," he said carefully. "That is the easiest way."

"I don't suppose I can wish I never picked this ring up."

"It would be...unpleasant, were you to do so." Fortunately, he did not have to say for whom.

Also fortunately, she did not ask.

"So, is my apartment going to be trashed all the time now? What am I supposed to do? Do I have to move? What the *fuck*?" An edge crept into her tone. Irritation, or anger.

It was heartening. "Mistress—" He stopped short, seeing her flinch. The small movement caused...discomfort. "Emily. I protect my bearer."

"Well, really, I only have your word for that." She dropped her hands, but she did not move to rearrange the ring. "Right?"

"You are still alive." It was logical enough, and he congratulated himself. Surely she would see reason. "Right?" It sounded different when he said it, though.

"For now." She took another step back, almost blundering into the couch. "Sure."

He stood, mute, as she turned away and headed for her bedroom.

"Christ." A tiny disbelieving laugh, just before she closed the door. "I can't even afford a hotel." She was rubbing at her tangled hair. The dust in it would no doubt begin to itch. Why hadn't he taken care of that when he restored her small home? It would have been no trouble, just as it would have been no trouble to smooth away the scratches.

That was not what she expressed a desire for, he told himself. *You are bound to that, and nothing else.*

He was also bound to truth, and he had not quite *lied.* What was he to do now, in the face of this numb retreat?

Nothing. It was all he *could* do, and that was a very unwelcome development indeed.

22

EMILY THE SAFE

HER PHONE BUZZED, AND THE TEXT POPPED UP. *WHAT THE fuck's up?* It was May, and she was probably concerned.

Emily's hair was still wet. Her scalp itched a bit, but maybe that was plaster.

Or *had* she washed the shampoo out? Taking a shower while jumping at every slight noise was a new and hideously uncomfortable experience. She even contemplated sleeping in her car, but what good would that do? Those big gray fuzzy things with the huge teeth, and their *faces*, shaped like dishes, the big raw open nose-holes...Jesus.

The more she thought about it, the more going nuts seemed almost better than magic and genies and long-furred, sniffing whatever-the-fucks. At least, with nuts, there was medication, right? There were places she could go and get put in a straitjacket.

Now *there* was a fun thought. Christ.

Emily made sure the charger was plugged in and settled back in the corner. It wasn't optimal, but when your apartment had been busted to shit and then zoom-la-di-da suddenly put back together, you had two choices: crawling under your bed and sleeping with the dust bunnies, or grabbing a pillow and a blanket and hiding in the closet.

She slid the mirrored door closed again, took a deep breath, and hunched over her phone. Work outfits, color-coded, hung happily on their wooden little homes. Although color-coded was kind of a misnomer, since she tended toward work clothes that would go with everything else she wore, just to be efficient. Three pairs of low black heels, two pairs of running shoes, one barely-used pair of hiking boots, and Dearfoam slippers still in their box for when her current pair wore out shared the closet floor with her. Cedar sachet hung on every third hanger, but it was still stuffy in here. And dusty.

I'm fine, her thumbs typed. *Bad day at work.*

That didn't even *begin* to cover it. Would May believe her? She typed *I have a genie in my living room*, then held down the delete key. Nope, that wouldn't do anything but make May laugh.

Deflection was the name of the game, then, until she could figure out how to get rid of the goddamn ring *and* stave off an incipient mental breakdown. She bit her lower lip and typed again.

Did you give my number to a stripper?

She could almost hear May's giggle when the answer came back. *Shit, did I give him yours? I meant to give him mine.*

On a normal day, she would have been able to guess whether May was joking or not. Today, though, her joke-o-meter was busted right down the middle and stomped flat for good measure. *So I should just give him yours when he calls again?*

There was a long pause, then her phone brightened and the tinkling notes of Tavares's "Heaven Must Be Missing An Angel" sounded, loud in the closet's confines. Em gasped, let it ring for a few seconds, then hit *accept.*

"Girl, you are just the worst!" May crowed, tinny through the speaker.

"So I've been told," Em mumbled, shutting her eyes against the darkness. *Pretend everything's fine. You're just tired.* Well, she was. "He sounds like a nice guy."

"Yeah, well, after you took a powder we partied with his crew. It was a blast, you should have stayed." Cheery, sunny, and chewing on something crunchy, May sounded just exactly like herself. It was a maddening consolation.

Yeah. I should have. "You know I'm no fun. So, listen, you want his number, or—"

"Try him out for me first?" Was that *hope* in her bestie's voice? Em squeezed her eyes shut even tighter. Hot water trembled, threatening to trickle between her lashes.

"Not gonna happen, May." *I have other things on my mind right now.*

That turned the conversation serious, and as usual, May jumped in with both feet. "You have got to get over Steven one of these days."

Oh, god DAMN it, no. "He's not the problem."

"Then what is?" It was the closest May would ever come to asking directly about the divorce.

We could just leave.

Em heard Steven's voice again, and felt the small internal motion that meant she had made a decision that was irrevocable and inconvenient all at once. "It's kind of late for this conversation on a weeknight."

"I get it, I get it, fine. Coffee tomorrow at the usual?"

She was about to say no, closing her eyes and breathing in the stale fusty scent of clothes hung and shut away, shoes waiting for their time in the sun, boxes of paperwork on the shelf above slowly accreting dust and exhaling the scent of bills, responsibilities, adulthood. There was no comfort in the darkness behind her eyelids *or* inside the closet.

"Yeah," she heard herself say. "I'd like that." *Maybe you can tell me if I'm crazy.* "May? Question."

"Huh?"

"Do you think I'm nuts?"

May thought about it for a few moments. "Honey, you are the most distressingly sane person I have ever met. That's why we're such a team." A scarf of bright laughter. "Ciao, love ya, ba-bye!"

Wait, Em wanted to say. *Notice something. Ask me why I'm in my closet instead of my living room. Tell me I sound strange. Something. Anything.*

She couldn't exactly *blame* May, really. They had their comfortable roles, like well-worn slippers. When was the last time they'd really talked about anything, well, *real?*

Emily the safe. Emily the sane. Emily the responsible, the designated driver, the one you called when you needed to know how to hire a plumber or do your taxes. Emily the straight arrow, Emily who had already married and divorced, doing it first so everyone else could relax. Even the divorce had been kind of bloodless. No real hurt feelings, just a distance. Emily, always doing the expected, the logical, the rational.

Emily the lonely. Emily the sitting in her closet, too afraid to sleep in her own bed.

I could call 911 right now and be carted away to the funny farm. I probably could make them take me; I could act crazy.

It would be an act, though. Like everything else, especially impersonating a responsible adult while she was just as scared and uncertain as her friends.

She dropped her phone and snuggled her bed's comforter around her. Sleeping sitting up in her closet had sounded good at the time, but her ass hurt and her legs were lying across shoes and her throat was full of something hot and rancid she denied.

Maybe it was fear. Or maybe it was the idea of the genie, standing in the middle of her living room. Was he sleeping on her couch? Did genies sleep?

Em tried, and tried again. The tears just lurked. They wouldn't come out, because she couldn't let her iron grip relax. She'd been shoving everything down and away so she could function for so long she *couldn't* break.

Finally, dry-eyed and pragmatic, she crawled out of the closet and into her bed, and fell into a thin, troubled slumber.

❦ 23 ❦
MOVED TO DO SO

THE WIND ROSE DURING THE NIGHT, FREEZING SMALL puddles into mirrors. The gray hush before dawn found Hal pacing barefoot and soundless from one end of her small living room to the other, occasionally drifting into the kitchen and scrutinizing every surface as if it might give him a solution to this strange discomfort.

Well, *discomfort* wasn't precisely the right word. *Distress* was closer. Why should it bother him so much to contemplate his mistress taking the ring off, perhaps with a curse? Left unprotected, she would return to a drab life, leered at by others like that hideous Brett man, for a short while before Cavanaugh's heirs or cohorts descended upon her.

Each time *that* thought reared its ugly head, he paused, whether on the linoleum in her entryway or kitchen, the carpet in the hall, or the much more used carpet in her living room. It scratched comfortingly against his soles, but it would not have garnered much praise in Cavanaugh's time. Rugs were meant to cushion and seduce, not to be purely utilitarian. Yet there were touches around the small flat that showed care and the instinct for beauty. Paintings reproduced and carefully framed, the small carvings on the bookshelf and scattered throughout the place. She had a fondness for turtles, and collected small figurines of them in whatever material caught her fancy. He had thought it a dingy nest for such a sweet-faced bird, but upon closer inspection, it was merely...subtle.

He did not want her to slip his fetter free.

What did it matter? One hand on his chains or another, he was still a servant. He felt the same pleasure whether he reassembled her destroyed furniture or made one of Cavanaugh's enemies choke to death on his own blood. Anything else had been taken from him, had it not?

Why was he so *hesitant*?

Several times he paced softly to the bedroom door, slipped into the subtle space of the insubstantial and slid through, hovering on the other side, straining his preternatural senses to catch her soft breathing. She slept as if she meant never to wake, perhaps finding a relief in unconsciousness. He did not dare to approach more closely, though none but the sharpest of unphysical senses could have discerned him.

What was the distress? He could not find it, so he paced.

The day strengthened outside. There was no whisper of another attack, no sign of another pursuit. Of course, when the dogs failed to return, the owners would turn suspicious. Which made it all the more imperative that he keep the ring on his new bearer's finger.

But *why*?

Could it be that he actually *preferred* one form of servitude to another? She was...engaging, this bearer. And somewhat kind, even if her language was shocking. A product of her time, perhaps. Had humanity grown a little gentler? It did not seem possible.

Hal found himself regarding the coffeepot on her wiped-clean counter. A neat and thrifty little soul, her dishes washed and set to dry, her cabinets methodically arranged.

Well, really, I have only your word for that.

Did she disbelieve the evidence of her own eyes, or had he been too slow and entirely too cavalier in dealing with the Appetites? She had been bruised and scraped. Had he moved to ease such things, though, she might very well have taken to screaming. That brittle calm might have broken.

What *could* he do? There had to be a solution. With all the resources at his command, helplessness was unthinkable.

Hal's gaze refocused on the coffee machine. Such a simple, elegant little thing. Whatever mortal had invented it had probably reaped much reward.

He heard her voice again, bright and cheerful. *I've had my eye on a sweet little espresso machine for a while, but it's a bit steep, you know? So I just have this Mr. Coffee but the beans are fresh.*

Could it be that simple?

There was nothing in the laws of his servitude that said he could not act of his own accord for his bearer's comfort instead of protection. He had rarely been moved to do so in the past.

Well, that was not quite accurate. He had *never* been moved in the past.

Hal turned sharply and paced for the larger room. There were glossy catalogs stacked neatly by size on the glass table crouching before her couch. Most had folded-down pages where something had caught her eye.

Those were desires. One could almost call them wishes.

I can't even afford a hotel, she'd said last night.

Wealth was easy. Comfort was seductive; women liked it, did they not? They had always seemed to, and his former bearers that wished to snare one started with gifts.

Perhaps he should give his new bearer a taste of his usefulness.

Hal found he was fully corporeal except for his right hand, which slid insubstantial through the pile of magazines, absorbing information. His face felt odd. Hal felt at his cheek with his fingertips, touched the corner of his lips. *That* was strange.

He was smiling.

HAL KNEW THE MOMENT SHE WOKE, BECAUSE SHE PUSHED herself up on her elbows and blinked fuzzily, her tumbled dark hair a halo. With her cheeks flushed and her shoulders bare except for the tiny straps of her camisole—you could not properly call such a scrap of clinging fabric a *shirt*—she was a vision. He should have immediately averted his gaze, but he did not have time.

His bearer frankly stared, her dark eyes huge, as the gray velvet window-curtains softly, slowly whispered wide, letting in first a few swords, then a flood of thin golden winter light. Her eyes widened further, and Hal let the light discover him by the new pale-pearl door with its gilt handle. Her bed was now dove-gray, a soft nest with pigeon-throat accents. Sheer netting fountained from a large ring set in the ceiling, the bed-nest safely held in a cloud; the carpeting was now the color of a sudden spring storm. A dainty white nightstand sat close with a lamp whose shade was jewel-bright mosaic glass, swans and heavy purple grapes intertwining.

Her mouth opened a little, showing those beautiful, pearly teeth. She stared at the walls, where her previous decorations —prints of some little quality—were now framed in lightly carved wood. A low padded bench at the end of her bed was just right for easing off her shoes at the end of a day, or putting them on at the beginning. Instead of her closet with its simple mirrored door, a wardrobe of fine cypress took up a very long wall that had not been there before—her bedroom was now much larger, and held two bookcases and a fantastical mirrored vanity with a cushioned bench, all of light lovely design.

He had not touched her clothes yet, though. He did not think a woman's temper would brook such a thing.

She blinked a few more times, and fished around in the covers for a small electronic device. The cell phones were *fascinating*, and he had very carefully made certain hers was in fine order as well as updated in a few small ways.

She thumbed the device, probably checking the time. Then she sat up, and the covers fell down to reveal the briefest of camisoles over her chest.

Hal decided to study the wardrobe. It was beautiful, even though he had simply guessed at what she would like. She had not found a proper wardrobe in any of her catalogs.

Finally, his bearer spoke.

"What." She coughed slightly, a little morning throat-clearing. "The fuck."

Was she pleased? He certainly hoped so. "I, ah. I took the liberty of...a few small..."

"It looks like a Munsters bordello in here." She rubbed at her forehead. Sleep-warm, tangled dark hair took new depth from the sunlight, chestnut and honey strands glowing in its richness. "And I'm late for work. Probably don't have a job anymore."

He brightened. "That is easily addressed, Mistress Emily. You are now the owner of several—"

"Dude." She fixed him with what would have been a stern look, if her hair had not been a most fetching bird's nest. "Mr. Genie. Hal." Well, at least she remembered his name on the third try. "I haven't had coffee yet, so keep this simple. What have you done to my bedroom?"

"I have...it is..." The speech he had prepared vanished,

leaving him floundering. "I, uh...Mistress Emily, I meant to... apologize."

She rubbed at her eyes with her free hand. A sigh filled her chest, and Hal found himself wondering if all the women of this time wore such things to bed. It was...distracting.

"Lord give me strength," she muttered, finally. Then she dropped her hand and regarded him levelly. "It's really nice, really it is." A hint of a pleased smile that did not seem very real touched her mouth, turning it into another distracting curve.

"But it does not please you?" He had an uncomfortable feeling that showing her the rest of the house just at this moment was perhaps a bad idea.

Her gaze sharpened, she pushed herself fully up to sit on the bed, and he hoped he had made the mattress of the right softness. "No, look, just...Jesus. Okay, look. Are we going to see any more of those things? From yesterday?"

That was a question he could answer with good grace. "Certainly not. I have taken some elementary precautions. This house is fully secure."

"House?" She shook her head when he began to explain. "No, no, really. Nope. Not just yet. I need caffeine." Her cell phone chirped, and she glanced at it. "Fuck. I'm late."

"For work?" He had planned to surprise her with freedom from that hideous maze of drudgery, but this conversation was *not* going as planned. If she would just put a few more layers of clothing on, he decided, it could easily be remedied.

"Well, I'm probably fired," she muttered darkly. "But no, I'm going to be late for coffee with May unless I get a move on." Emily dropped her hands, and regarded him steadily. "So those things won't come back?"

"They will not." *Or I will attend to them.*

"Do you promise?" She slid for the side of the bed, and despite the care with which he had transmuted the sheets and blankets around her sleeping form, he could not tell if she was wearing anything other than the camisole.

"I do," he managed. There was some kind of obstruction in his throat.

Two slim bare feet, two long, pale, lightly muscled legs, and he found out she wore breeches cut indecently short to allow freedom of movement. What in the world had happened to nightgowns, as the women of Cavnaugh's time wore? This display was... He had never, *never* had this manner of reaction to a bearer before.

"You made a whole house? With all my stuff?" She picked her way over the carpet, graceful as a gazelle, plucking at the camisole and the small breeches to arrange them more comfortably on her frame. Her breasts moved slightly with every step, just like her curls.

"Each of your possessions is safely..." He lost the thread of the sentence, for her knee was still scratched. There was a gemming of dark blood-beads along it, and it occurred to him that he had not repaired *that*, as he should have. He made a lunging effort to remember what he was saying, his hands itching to move, to touch the scrape and see it vanish along with the dark bruise on her thigh and the one on her right arm. "Safely here. Your chariot—your *car*, everything."

"Holy wow." She stopped, turned in a complete circle, gazing at the bedroom. There was her battered red alarm clock, a little out of place on the beautiful white nightstand. The prints were still hers, and a fuzzy pink bathrobe was folded neatly on the vanity's bench, with her almost-thread-bare slippers tucked underneath. "You did all this while I was sleeping. Crazy."

"You are quite sane." He had no idea what else to say. The breeches hid almost nothing, and he denied himself the urge to look at the fascinating portion of her midriff he could see, the flare of her hindquarters, the—

"I've been that way all my life." Her lip faintly curled, as if she considered it a highly dissatisfying state of being. "But you know what, Hal-the-Genie, my man? I'm beginning to think it's overrated." Her phone chirped again. "Jesus *Christ*," she said. "I gotta get going. Please tell me you didn't mess with my clothes."

"Indeed, I did not—"

"Great. Uh...where *are* my clothes?"

He pointed at the wardrobe, and found himself watching the sway of her hips as she stalked for it, poking at her phone with her thumb and muttering various imprecations. His jaw was suspiciously loose. He had not expected... By the Ring, how did mortal men *bear* it? Was this what made them chase the fairer half? He had no recollection of suffering this... distraction...in the dim, gray time before his transformation.

She stopped halfway, glanced over her shoulder at him. "I'm gonna get dressed, do you mind?"

I most certainly do not mind at all. "Ah. Um, no." He felt for the doorhandle behind him, and just as she lifted the hem of the camisole, meaning to strip it off over her head, he staggered back through the door and shut it with a bang, without even the sense to slide into insubstantiality.

❦ 24 ❦

MANY PRINCIPLES

EMILY BLINKED, SHADING HER EYES WITH ONE HAND. IT wasn't just a house. It was a gigantic whipped-cream pile of overblown Taj Mahal, with a huge honking helping of stained glass. *Oh, hell no.* But when she brought her chin back down, she found the genie studying her face, and he looked a little...

Well, he looked like a kid really proud of his macaroni artwork but suspecting it wasn't up to snuff. Even though his mouth was pulled as tight as ever and his hair was all slicked back, his nose was high and proud, and his almost-ugly cheek-bones too, a tiny fleeting motion around his dark eyes gave Em a definite sense of uneasy pity.

"Do you like it?" He even sounded *eager,* for God's sake. Like an elementary school kid showing you his art, hoping for a good reaction.

"It's very...big. It's nice," she added hastily. "And in Grant Park, too. That's a good address." *The neighbors are probably furious. Do you think they even notice?* She refrained from asking by sheer force of will.

Her Honda looked very small on the tar-black, circular driveway, but it was gleaming as if it had been freshly waxed.

The genie meekly got into the passenger's seat when she told him to, and she had a moment of dry-mouth irrationality before she could open the driver's side door. She put the key in the ignition, buckled her seat belt, and paused. "Look, don't do that disappearing shit, okay? Not while I'm driving. Try not to startle me."

"Yes, mistress."

Lord help me, I'm in an I Dream of Jeannie reboot. "Just...call me Emily, okay?" In the center of the driveway was a statue that looked vaguely familiar, until she realized she'd seen it at the museum. A Waldroup sculpture in blue metal of a man sitting hunched over, his hand to his head, the lines more fluid than metal should be. The piece breathed resignation and sadness, but it was beautiful, and she'd folded down the page it was on in the museum catalog.

Good God. The sense of being in a dream returned, but she didn't think pinching herself was a good idea.

"Yes, Emily." Again, just like a kid. Anxious to please. Hopeful.

Oh, goddammit. She reached for the key again, stopped. "I, uh...look, I was really upset last night. I'm still not too happy about this, but...well, you seem like a nice person. You know? You seem...nice." *Is that all I can say?*

That earned her a long, considering look. His chin wasn't as big as she'd thought before, really, and if he got a haircut his face probably wouldn't look so...weird. A ghost of a smile touched his tight-drawn lips. "Thank you, Emily."

"I mean, I'm probably crazy, but if I have to be bazonko nuts, you're not bad company." *Though I hardly know anything about you.*

"Thank you." That ghost of a smile strengthened a little. "Emily? May I touch your wrist?"

Say what? "Uh." Her hands were on the wheel, and she

darted a glance at the car door. "Sure, I guess. Thank you for asking."

He reached over, and two fingertips touched the back of her hand.

Em gasped. Warm electricity traveled down her arm, tingled in her fingertips, bolted down her aching side and turned hot on her scraped knee. When he took his hand away, the various aches and nips of pain from last night's tango with the big hairy things had vanished, and the looming caffeine-withdrawal headache had retreated. "Wow. What was *that?*"

"I should have attended to your hurts last night. I am... sorry, that I did not."

"Oh. Okay." She twisted the key, the engine woke, and she let out a long breath, bracing herself. "Thank you. That's, ah, very kind of you. Put your seat belt on."

"What?"

"Your seat belt." She pulled the strap of her own away from her chest, let it go. The idea of checking to see if the bruise was still on her arm from whapping her bathroom's threshold was almost overwhelming, but she'd had all the weird she could take just at the moment. *I am doing okay with this. Doing really well. Sort of.* "Put it on. In case there's a crash."

"I cannot be harmed by—" He stopped, shut his mouth with a snap, still watching her. "Is that a command?"

For Chrissake. "No, it's just a basic precaution. Please put your seat belt on, Mr. Hal." It took him a moment, but he figured it out, and when it clicked home Emily nodded. "Thank you. I mean, it doesn't mean a lot when there's magic, but it's the principle of the thing."

"Do you have many principles, Mistress Emily?"

She dropped the car into drive. "Well, we're about to find

out. Having a genie is probably an acid test for ethics, you know."

"Is that what you wish to call me? A genie?"

"What would you call it?"

He didn't say anything. The Honda crept cautiously for that huge iron gate, which opened as smooth as silk, the E in the middle suddenly, uncomfortably bisected. *Man, this guy doesn't do anything halfway, does he.*

"Mistress Emily." Almost prissily formal. "I have not had many...*principled*...bearers."

"Oh." *Well, crap.* It was amazing none of them had nuked the world, for God's sake. "Guess I'm going to have to be the first, then." She pulled out onto Forest Park Way, one of the most expensive and narrowest streets in the whole damn city, and tried to remember how to get downtown.

"YOU'RE LATE." MAY PEERED OVER HER HEART-SHAPED sunglasses, one hip hitched artfully on a high barstool. Caprasano's Coffee didn't have many tables, and the ones they *did* have you had to climb on mismatched barstools to get to. The place took hipster to new heights, but they roasted the beans on-site and their pastries were works of art. The place smelled of coffee, baked goods, diets blown to smithereens and tubs of chocolate gleefully rubbed all over naked skin.

Well, maybe not the last one, but it was close.

Emily set her purse on the postage-stamp table and unwound her sober, sensible, navy blue knitted scarf. *I had to explain the concept of paid parking to a genie.* "Rough night."

"Isn't that my line?" Her best friend's cherry-glossed lips pursed, and the scrutiny quickly became uncomfortable. Two lattes—one hazelnut, one ginger, and they always took sips of each others'—sat there, only a little past steaming. The traditional plain croissant—Emily's—and *pain au chocolat*—May's—sat on sugar-dusted plates, and for a moment, it was like being fresh out of college and starving again, both of them pooling tips or whatever quarters they could scrounge out of someone else's couch cushions to pay for a shared entree somewhere nice. "What's wrong?"

"Just..." Emily glanced at the plate-glass window stretching along Fourth Street. "Nothing. Life. That sort of shit."

I can be invisible, the genie had said. *I will merely watch, to protect you.*

Her left thumb touched the warm silver band of the ring, pressed against her sweating palm.

May made a small beeping noise and pushed her sunglasses up like a headband, sweeping coppery hair away from her face. Today it was purple glitter eyeliner and striped tights, a knee-length plaid skirt and white buttondown with a vest that belonged in a prep school. She was wearing her oxfords, too, and an unwontedly serious expression. She would probably be able to pull off Catholic-schoolgirl schtick until the day she died. "Wrong answer. You've been out of signal since the party. What happened?"

I fell into a fairy tale. "I just got too drunk. Depressed, I guess." Emily clambered onto her own barstool and pretended interest in her latte. "You know, just life. Plus this cowboy stripper keeps calling me, which I know *you* have something to do with."

For once, May didn't have a snappy comeback. She actually flushed, looking at her own rapidly cooling latte, and the guilty expression was so new that for a moment Emily thought maybe the whole thing was an elaborate prank and May was going to come clean, tell her how her drinks were spiked, and ask for forgiveness. *We rigged your apartment—*

Bert's a real whiz with lights, you know, and we dressed up some of the guys as werewolves. Crazy, huh?

"So yeah," May finally said, pushing her plate away a fraction of an inch and turning even redder. "About that. I, uh... you're gonna kill me."

"Now why would I do that?" The sinking sensation in her stomach wouldn't go away. It *couldn't* be a prank, could it?

What did it mean that she was suddenly hoping it wasn't?

"Well...I offered him...to, uh, give you a...a private date, sort of." May fidgeted on her seat, her fingers jumping like little mice. "I thought, you know, he was supposed to take you home and..."

Emily blinked several times, willing the situation to make sense inside her skull. "You...bought me a boy hooker?"

"No! Nothing like that, he wasn't... But I said you were repressed and... Christ, Em, I thought it wouldn't kill you to have a date and he was so nice, he said he understood and—"

"You paid someone to take me on a date?" *I can't decide whether to be relieved or kind of insulted.* "Wait. You paid a Canadian stripper to ask me on a date?"

"He's Canadian?" May looked horrified.

Emily suppressed the desire to put her head down on the tiny table and burst into helpless laughter. Frankly, there wasn't room. "From Ontario. Did you miss that bit?"

"I didn't *pay* him. I just said, you know, you should take my friend out. And he said he'd be happy to, because not everyone could pull off Elvira, and—"

"You asked a stripper to..." Her voice shook. "Only you, May. Christ Jesus, only you."

"Don't be mad. It's just that, ever since Steven—"

"Can we not bring Steven into this?" Laughter won, just barely. Emily clapped a hand over her mouth, rolled her eyes, and tried to hold back the flood.

"Oh, God." May's blue eyes shone with tears. "Please,

please don't be mad. I just thought you could use a little, you know—"

Emily waved her free hand, desperately. Her stomach hurt, her own eyes blurred. May probably thought it was fury, because she went dead white except for the crimson patches on her cheeks. It took a while for her best friend to figure out Emily was laughing as messily and completely as a child.

"I just thought you deserved a nice *time!*" she kept saying, and that sent Emily into fresh cascades of relieved merriment. It was just the sort of alcohol-laced, hilarious generosity May was prone to. At least Ontario Cowboy hadn't mentioned Emily just *vanishing*.

That would have been awkward.

Finally, dabbing at her eyes with a napkin, Emily regained some kind of control. Some of the other customers were glancing uneasily at their table, and normally that might have mortified her. Today, though, her mortification-meter was pretty well absent. "Okay." She managed not to go into a fresh spate of giggles. Her stomach hurt. "Good Lord. Wow."

"He's really a nice guy. Saving up for when he goes home, he said. We had a big long conversation, and..." May twisted her own napkin into a fraying rope, a sure sign of nervousness. "You're not mad? I really...Don't be mad, okay?"

"I'm *amused*." Somewhat grimly amused, but she didn't have to tell May as much. "I wondered why he was calling, that's all. You had a long conversation?"

"We both like eighties cartoons. You remember that one with the guy who had the emerald ring, and he and his friends were fighting off giant plants?"

Not at all. "Vaguely."

"Well, he knew the title." May's grin, a little tremulous, was gathering strength. "And we talked about She-Ra and He-Man and Care Bears and—"

Aha. Hang on just one cotton-picking second. "Sounds like you like him."

"Oh, no." Instant disagreement. But the lady was protesting a little *too* much. "He's not my type. I thought some no-strings-attached might be good for you, and he asked for my number but I gave him yours and said you could use a date—"

"Christ, am I really that pathetic?" Em shook her head. "Don't answer that."

"You're not pathetic. But if you keep locking yourself up and refusing to have any fun your hymen's going to grow back, and who needs that shit?" May kept twisting the napkin. "So...has he been calling you?"

Huh. She really *likes him.* "Once or twice. I couldn't talk, I was at work—"

"Work?" May looked perplexed. "Okay, that's new, when did you get a job?"

I've been working since I was fourteen. "I..." *Wait a second. The genie.*

She hadn't had him explain just *what* he'd done to her apartment, and it looked like he'd made a few other changes, too. Great. "I like to be useful," she said, hoping it was vague enough to pass muster. "Anyway, I was driving, so I didn't get a chance to chat. But I'll call him."

"You will?" May's face went through three or four lightning-fast flickers of expression, one after another, settling on a neutral smile. "Good, that's good. Tell him I said hello."

"I will." Em's brain had begun to work again, and a few things were fitting together. *Oh, will I ever.* "So. I feel like I haven't seen you in ages. Tell me everything." Hopefully, she could pick up a few things around the edges of her best friend's chatter. She should have thought to question the damn genie more closely.

"Well." May settled on her barstool, confident again. "So,

the party. Omar found Andy and Bert necking in one of the bedrooms, and there was a knock-down drag-out that only ended when Gloria shouted them both down because *Omar*, you see, has discovered his hetero side again with June—Pascal, not that bitch Diamanti—and Glo knew about it. It's a good thing the strippers were all so big and burly, because they had to keep everyone separated—"

"Holy crap." Well, she didn't have to feel bad about seeing Andy and Bert on the deck and keeping her mouth shut, then. And May was right: the Diamanti woman was a grade-A twatsicle. "Guess I left at just the right time."

"I guess so." May didn't look envious at all. If there was one thing she loved, it was a good session of telling poor old bewildered Em all the gossip. "And Gwynnie—that dishwater blonde with the horrible tattoos—was acting like she was going to pass out, so someone called an ambulance—"

Emily kept nodding and making the right noises, letting the chatter flow around her. All the time, she was busy planning—and making a list of questions for the genie, once May had her fill of attention.

NO WAY OF TELLING

HAL HOVERED UNCERTAINLY AT THE WINDOW. THEIR GLASS was of very fine quality, and there was so *much* of it. The luxury was utterly taken for granted, and he wondered if he had overlooked some small but critical items last night. She *seemed* pleased enough, but had insisted on leaving her car in a gigantic concrete building full of similar conveyances, the floors stacked atop each other high enough to make any mortal dizzy.

Just don't get in any trouble, she'd told him before entering this small coffeehouse. She said she would pay to retrieve her car when she was done, and his immediate offer to make such a thing unnecessary had been politely but firmly declined.

She said *please.* And *thank you.* And *I am asking you.* No commands. Simple requests.

Why?

Breeches of some soft clinging fabric, a black shirt that clung to her as well, and the only thing saving him from considering striking every mortal man who passed blind was the length of her woolen coat. Her blue knitted scarf made her skin look even softer in comparison, and though more than one man glanced at her, none of them outright stared.

That was good, for Hal was not certain he...

What was he *thinking*? What his bearers wore was of no concern.

He watched, hungrily, as the redheaded mortal woman leaned forward, twisting her napkin into a rope for emphasis. At first Hal had thought his bearer was weeping; the urge to sweep into the coffee shop and discover the source of her agitation had almost overwhelmed him.

But no. She *laughed*. Her eyes outright danced, her curls bounced, and Hal found himself queerly breathless. At least, he *felt* breathless, though he was incorporeal at the moment. What had amused her so? He could drift inside and listen, could he not?

But perhaps she would not wish him to?

His hesitation was new. How had the world changed so much? Had he really thought everything would continue in the same well-worn groove while he was trapped in the castle? Wonders rode the air here, from the giant silvery birds carrying mortals in their bellies far above to the glowing screens they watched and tiny devices they spoke or tapped into to communicate. His own abilities did not exactly pale in comparison, and yet he was suddenly, irrationally afraid they might.

At least, for *her*. She did not seem eager to command. Had humanity changed so much? By now her head should be spinning with possibilities; she should be drunk with sudden capability. Perhaps he had simply not shown her enough.

The—what do you call them? Her forehead had furrowed before she shook her head to forestall his reply. *Appetites. Right. The Appetites were certainly an eyeful, Hal.*

That was a problem. If the Fratres were still robust

enough to send such things after his ringbearer, they were more than able to send *other* hunters. How far would they go to regain possession of his fetter? Could he make it unprofitable enough to dissuade them? And, of course, keep her mostly unaware at the same time. Her reaction last night had been...troubling.

Here he was, actively seeking to keep his fetter on a bearer's finger. A *woman*, of all things. One who had less use for him than she did for her tiny handheld telephone, another wonder of the modern world. He almost wanted to smash the devices, or cripple the soundless waves they depended on.

Now the redhead was talking very rapidly, and his bearer was listening. Did the other woman not see the faint pained expression on Emily's face? Did she not suspect his bearer's shoulders were tight with strain, and she only toyed with the small, exquisite pastry before her? Small sips of her drink—he should be there to test it for poison. Cavanaugh's fellow Fratres had more than once tried to dislodge him with venom.

He needed to know their dimensions now, their new methods. Perhaps they had changed with the times as well. If he took his attention elsewhere, though, there might be another attack, and his bearer unprotected during it.

At least if one of *them* held his fetter, they would know how to use him. He could settle back into the half-malicious watchfulness, obeying the letter of the commands and leaving the spirit untouched as it pleased him. He would not feel this...uncertain.

Finally, the redhead chattered herself to a standstill, exchanged air-kisses with his bearer, and hurried out as if she had another appointment. Hal spread his insubstantial self across the pavement in front of the window, but she turned the other way, tipping her plastic spectacles with darkened lenses down over her eyes. She bounced along, as if relieved of a heavy weight.

Emily was left to clean the remains of the pastries from the table, and drop her nearly untouched drink into the dustbin. The sheer amount of rubbish they produced nowadays was only rivaled by the receptacles they had engineered to hold it. His bearer even took a few fresh paper scraps and wiped the table they had been at, despite the fact that it was obviously the job of the coffeehouse workers. She did not look sad, merely thoughtful, her dark curls tumbling every which way though she had made more than one attempt to hold them back during the conversation. There were shadows under her large dark eyes, and Hal resolved out of invisibility, resting his boots against the cracked concrete and deciding not to press his nose to the glass, no matter how fine of a quality it was.

If he simply appeared next to her as she exited, it might... frighten her.

Why do you care? What are you doing?

Perhaps his long sojourn in the castle had disturbed some crucial balance, and he was slightly mad. There was no way of telling, especially when you held such power. When you could warp the very fabric of what mortals called *reality*, what was to stop you from growing...strange?

The small bell on the door jingled as his mistress stepped outside. She shivered a little, pulling her jacket more closely about her, and saw him. Her expression didn't change much, but her shoulders tensed still further, as if taking on another burden.

Ah. Much about her now became clear. He would wager his soul, did he have such a thing left after the operation to bind him to the ring, that she had listened to her friend's troubles and volunteered none of her own.

"Hey." She moved out of the doorway, tilting her chin up

to look at him. "Were you there the whole time? It's cold out here."

"I do not feel it." *And you should not, either.*

Before he could add that remark, though, she shook her head and smiled wearily. The kindness in the expression, however, threatened to still his breath. "Well, May's all right now. So we can talk about you."

What? "What?"

"About you. What makes you comfortable, how we're going to get you free."

"Free?" The sensation of the world slipping away from underneath his feet troubled him. Had he gone incorporeal with shock?

"Isn't that what every genie wants? You're basically a slave, and that's not *right*, dammit. There's no reason you should have to do just what any goddamn yahoo who picks up the ring tells you." She brushed past him, and somehow her arm threaded through his. "You have rights. This is America."

Hal found himself walking quite naturally with his bearer, her arm through his, and stopped. "That is *not* right." A moment's worth of concentration and he was on her other side, remembering that a gentleman walked nearest the street to save his companion from peril—and, not so incidentally, from mud that would foul her skirts. Though she wore those strange trousers, which hid nothing of her long legs *or* her... her hindquarters. "There, better."

"Why did you—"

"A gentleman walks to the street, Emily. And I do not mind working my bearer's will." *At least, I do not mind working yours.*

She glanced at him, her forehead wrinkling as if his state-ment troubled her. "But when I get the ring off, or when I—"

"You will not take the ring off." He did not mean it to sound so declarative. *I am walking. With a mortal woman. Who knows what I am.* A pleasant thrill ran down his nerves. "Yet there is something...are you familiar with history?"

"I went to college," she replied, somewhat stiffly. The brisk damp breeze brought color to her cheeks, and made her curls move gently.

"Do you think, Mistress Emily, that you could solve a mystery for me?"

Her expression eased. Interest, and relief. "What mystery's that?"

"My...former bearer." He congratulated himself for redirecting her so neatly. She liked to help. Her mortal friends probably inundated her with requests for advice, and she probably let them. "I am...curious, as to what happened to him."

She thought this over, glancing down at her shoes as if she trusted him to steer her safely. "Did you like him?"

"No." He did not bother lying. It was pleasant, to feel her corporeal weight against his. And *very* pleasant to think an onlooker would see a man walking with his... He brought his attention back to the matter at hand. "But something troubles me about last night's visitors."

"You think they might be—wait a second. Do you...maybe he's still alive? If he wished for, you know, immortality?"

"He desired the closest thing I could grant to that, yes." Next, he thought, she would enquire further as to the mechanics of *that* gift.

"And he gave up the ring, maybe?" She glanced down, at her left hand. His fetter gleamed, and he wondered if he dared to seal it to her flesh, to make *certain* she could not take it off until he willed as much. "So it's possible."

"That is what troubles me." *Among other things.* "It is perhaps *possible* but not very *likely.*"

"So maybe he was...killed? While you weren't around to stop it?"

"He was an exceeding cautious individual." *As well as an exceedingly vicious one.*

"Even cautious people can end up dead." She sucked in her lips, another thoughtful expression, and Hal frowned. The crowd on the sidewalk was a little difficult to navigate, unless he moved them slightly aside. He did not wish to be jostled. Did she shudder, and lean a little more upon his arm?

Not you, my bearer. "Indeed. There is much I can learn just from absorption, but I wish to know precisely what happened to him. Do you think it possible?"

Silence for a long moment. Did she notice they walked in their own slice of space, people turning a few fractions aside ahead to give plenty of room?

If she did, she made no mention of it. "Well, it's worth a try. If we figure out how *he* got the ring off, there might be hope yet."

Are you so ready to be rid of me? What more did she want? "Do I displease you, Mistress Emily?"

That brought her chin up and her gaze to rest on his face. Or his profile, since he watched the sidewalk before them, smoothing any stray irregularity that could trip her. "Of course not. You're a little weird, but I think you're a nice guy. And I was wondering..."

"What?" So there was something she would ask for, after all. Something in Hal's chest felt strange.

"Well, there's that guy from Ontario. I met him the night you...well, Halloween." Her eyes had begun to sparkle.

His stomach tightened. "Yes?" Would she ask him to ensnare a lover for her? All mortals were the same, selfish and short-sighted, greedy and ungracious.

"And it strikes me that he and my friend May might need a little help."

What? His own feet almost tangled. "Help?"

"Tell me, Hal my man." Now it was not merely her eyes;

her entire face had lit up, flushed with interest and something approaching happiness. And if his physical form had not a deep and abiding need to breathe, he might have lost said breath entirely and never regained it. "How are you at playing matchmaker?"

❦ 26 ❦

EARLY ENOUGH FOR CHURCH

"A *WOMAN*." THE OLD MAN SHOOK HIS HEAD, THE BULB AT the end of his nose twitching again. "Inconceivable."

It was the third time he'd said it, and the urge to say *I don't think that means what you think it means* almost choked Peter each time. Nobody here would get the reference, though, and it was a lot safer to keep his mouth shut until he was sure he could speak without laughing nervously. The gas insert fire danced merrily, and the lights were dimmed for the old man's vanity. Electric bulbs tended to be too bright for a man who had grown up with candles.

"I felt it quite clearly." Bruce Vance was pale, but holding up admirably. His facility for such work was outstanding, and thought-provoking, since it flew in the face of the old man's considered opinion that talent sprang from good breeding.

Vance was also, Peter thought, grateful to be given a chance or two. Which made him very useful indeed. The talented among the lower classes were always hungry to obey. Vance had made an attempt to get his suits tailored, and it showed. Perhaps Peter should give him some advice.

The small parlor at Peakes End was paneled in oak and

very cozy, but it smelled like it had been closed for a while. Which it had been. After all, Vance was a plebeian, and it was beyond the old man to let such an insect into the *large* parlor. This one, with its thick red carpet and almost-modern sideboard—though there would be no *good* booze in it, just the cheap sort—was far more fitting for the occasion.

"Women cannot..." The old man sighed, pinching the bridge of his nose with his unmutilated right hand. "Well, the world has degenerated. I don't know why I am surprised."

Rich Greene and Grosvenor the mayor's helper were at home, nursing the peculiar almost-hangover that came with working with the invisible. Maggs, Moss, and Sampson, dead-eyed and hollowed out, had shuffled away when the old man dismissed them. Each of them looked thinner, less...substantial. Maggs's spray tan turned him orange as Cheeto dust, because he was so pale underneath it. Their wives and families might notice something was off, but would probably chalk it up to overwork. Except in Dick Sampson's case—he was divorced, which was a surprise to exactly nobody who had seen him and the missus together in public. *She* was in an entirely different pay grade, and sometimes Peter had thought about following up on some of the long, speculative looks he had pretended not to notice her throwing in his direction.

Maybe later, once the rest of this affair was dealt with. The hilt pressing into his lower back was a comforting reminder that it wouldn't be long. He took care to keep his tone even. "She may not know what she has."

"Or she thinks she's going insane." Vance's gaze was direct, forthright, and altogether a little disturbing. "*And* she doesn't know what she has."

"I would not put it past that lying sprite to mislead a *woman*." The old man's left hand turned into a fist, the stump of his index finger jutting out obscenely. His thronelike leather chair, pulled close to the fire, was subtly turned to exclude both Peter and Bruce. The lord of the manor, at once deigning to speak and retaining control of the conversation. "And now he will be on his guard." He glanced at Peter. "What do we do when an opponent is on his guard?"

The old answer was strike where he does not expect, but Peter was tired of parroting the old lines. "Redirect. Move into the blind spot. Adapt." *The world has changed, Great-great-however many grandfather. And you haven't. Much.*

Although the old man had probably been a pretty effective bastard in his day. Now he was a liability, and a snake-dangerous one.

The bulb on the old man's nose broadened and twitched once as his thin lips stretched into a grin that did not reach his eyes. New answers were sometimes greeted with disdain, or worse, punishment. Since the old man was counting on Peter to bring replacement members into the fold, though, a little bit of pushing was acceptable.

If the old bastard got his hands on that ring, the story would change, quickly.

"Exactly." The old man's tone was avuncular, kind, and extremely dangerous. He shook out his damaged hand, and Peter found himself wondering if the missing finger hurt sometimes. Phantom pain was a bitch for amputees. "Mister Vance, you have performed well indeed. Go home, get some rest."

"Sir." Vance glanced at Peter again as he rose, a brief, inscrutable look. He even closed the door softly on his way out. It was pretty likely he knew this was the smaller parlor, and that he knew why it had been chosen.

He might have been a plebe, but no moss grew on him. And Peter had taken care to appear his ally, as well as the one man in the inner circle who didn't snub him in the general meetings.

"Well, Peter, my boy." The old man sighed. "Let us retire for the evening. Tomorrow is early enough for church."

Church? The floor, perfectly steady, threatened to shift under his feet. "You're going to use *them?*"

"Who better?" Damn the asshole, he even looked *pleased.* At least, his eyes had begun to sparkle. But he still rubbed at his mutilated left hand, thoughtfully and with a slightly obscene milking motion. "Oh, my boy. You never disappoint. Let's have a nightcap before bed, shall we?"

✀ 27 ✀

IF SOMEONE MAKES YOU

"Hello?" He sounded a little breathless. "Don't hang up, I'm here, please don't hang up."

Em had plastered a wide, fake smile to her face. It was habit, when you had to talk on the phone to clients or anyone you wanted to fool. She plugged her other ear with a fingertip, and hoped he could hear her. "Well, hello there. Is this Toronto's most famous cowboy stripper?"

"By night, yes." He had a nice mellow tenor, too. "By day I'm a penniless student, but thanks for asking."

"Man of many talents. So you know who this is." *If you don't I'm going to feel a little silly.*

"Sort of. You're the disappearing lady."

Em winced. Just what *did* he remember? And what would the genie do about it if she told him she suspected a stripper suspected?

Of course, the stripper probably didn't suspect. "One of *my* many talents." She examined the genie's blue-clad shoulder, pressing into her free ear more firmly so she wouldn't yell into the receiver. The rain was holding off and there wasn't much of a breeze, but right outside the Metropolitan Library wasn't the best place for peace and quiet; it would be obvious that she was outside. "I just had coffee with a certain redheaded lady who solved the mystery of how you got my digits."

"Yeah. Look, about that…"

She waited, but he very little else to say. There was noise on his end, too—someone yelling something, a brief blurring sound of something being nailed or stapled. She decided to go back on the offensive. "Chill, it's all copacetic. Look, I'd really like to talk to you. Can we do coffee? Say, Thursday at eleven AM?"

"Um." He sounded unsure. "I really…"

She looked up at the genie, her eyebrows raised. He nodded, fractionally, a brief odd flash in his dark eyes.

"Sure!" Jake the Toronto Cowboy Stripper said. "Where?"

Another instance of a few moments' worth of planning being better than a pound of thinking on your feet. Em's grin widened, and it felt natural now. "At La Almeda on Fortieth. You know it?"

"It's that coffee shop with the firebreather on its sign?"

Fitting, isn't it? You have no idea how much. "The very same, right next to the Barnes Mutual building. I'll see you there."

"Okay, but I have to tell you—"

Oh, no you don't. She hung up, and peered up at the genie. "Okay. Now, May pretty much always goes there on her lunch break. I just need you to get her there a little earlier on Thursday, at eleven instead of noon. Can you do that without causing an explosion or losing her job or anything?"

"I can be exceedingly subtle." Another brief nod. "And do you wish him there as well?"

Duh. "Well, I invited him. You think he won't show up?"

"Would you like to be sure?" His head moved, slowly, he gazed down at her like she was speaking Swahili or something. "And do you wish them to fall in love?"

I'll settle for some short-term lust to make her happy and distract her at the same time. Em blinked, glancing at the sky. Dark clouds hovered to the north; normally they would be knee-deep in snow already. Winter was damn mild this year. "Uh, well, that's sort of not...no, I think things will be, uh, happen naturally if we just get them together. Love's a big word, they're definitely in *like*."

He considered this, a few strands of his dark ponytail moving on the breeze. He'd positioned himself to block most of the wind coming down Fifteenth. Awful nice of him. "But would you like to be *sure*? I can fill them with desire for each other."

Whoa. "I think that's pretty much already happened. He's been trying to tell me nicely each time that he's only calling me to get May's number. It's a shame, because he's packed and stacked, but—"

The genie's expression darkened slightly. "Do you wish him to fall in love with *you*, then?"

Christ no. I'm too busy for anything else now that you've shown up. Besides, the idea sent a hot bolt of distaste crawling up from her stomach. "Hell no. Why the fuck would I want something like *that*?"

Behind Hal, the granite facing of the library was full of muted color. His blue sweater didn't look nearly thick enough to keep him warm. "Your...friend. She is not overcaring of you, I thought perhaps a manner of revenge could be—"

"May's my best friend." Her tone could best be described as *warning*, and Em shivered as the dark fringe of cloud slid over the already veiled sun.

"She is selfish and thoughtless."

Oh, hell no, magical dude. You do not get to make snap judgments about my friends. That's my job. "You don't know a goddamn thing about her, so just..." She restrained herself from saying *shut up* just in time. Took a deep breath, just as a spatter of icy rain rattled against the Library's granite facade. It was going to be a cold, wet afternoon. "Let's not get sidetracked. We're here to do some research about your former, um, boss."

"Master."

"*Boss*." The urge to glare at him was rising. "And yes, I would like both May and Toronto Stripper at the coffee shop at the same time. But no funny stuff, okay? Just...get them there, and let things take their course."

"Why is that acceptable, and filling them with desire not?" He even sounded genuinely curious. He didn't look like the cold bothered him at all.

"Because it's not the same if someone *makes* you do it." Although, really, was getting them to the coffee shop together a step over the ethical boundary? "Crap." She exhaled, a long sound of frustration. "Look, you can't just force people to shag, or to fall in love. You really can't. All you can do is give an opportunity. They'll figure it out. At the very worst they share an uncomfortable ten minutes talking about me and May goes back to work and he goes back to school, and I admit to May that I told him where to find her. But the rest of it's just... Jesus. Did your other, um, bearers, did they do shit like that?"

"Your language is extraordinary." A dismissive flick of his dark head. Somehow the rain avoided him. There wasn't even a droplet on his lean shoulders, for Chrissake. "They were men, and thought to take their due. Women were to be sought, and had."

Ewwww. Misogyny central. "I like these guys less and less. And you just...you just did it?"

"I had no choice." He'd gone from curious to remote in a heartbeat, his thin face slamming shut with an almost audible snap. "What the bearer desires, I must perform."

It was on the tip of her tongue to ask if any of the bearers had, well, tastes that leaned toward *his* type too. It was a distinctly uncomfortable notion, and that wasn't the sort of thing you asked someone. *They were men,* he said, just like someone else would say *the sky is blue.*

And May wondered why she didn't date. Come to think of it, was she doing May any favors by putting her together with this guy both of them barely knew?

Em's stomach grumbled a little. She should have eaten her croissant. In a little bit she'd get cranky, and she was under-caffeinated as well. "Christ." Another sigh welled up inside her. "Well, what I'm desiring right now is lunch, some decent espresso, and finding out what happened to your last boss. But *you* don't have to do a thing about it. Come on, and be quiet. The last thing I need is to be thrown out of a library."

"I would not let them, Mis—ah, Emily."

Comforting. "Thanks." She had to push past him to get around a fluted column—the library was part of a super-Edwardian pomp and neoclassical circumstance; you could practically smell the railroad baron who built it and his greasy, hair-pomaded satisfaction. "Let's get on the internet."

"First stop is always Google." She pointed at the chair next to her at the long table, unwrapping her scarf. The computers weren't too crowded this early in the afternoon, and thank goodness he'd caught on about speaking very softly. The librarians in here were serious business.

The genie settled gingerly, glancing over the bookshelves with longing written on his face. Then he turned his chin back toward her, the very picture of patient attention.

So she had to ask. "Do you like reading?"

"I can absorb a great deal from books. From your electronics, not so much. Yet."

Now *that* was interesting. "Yet?"

"I will adapt." He said it so grimly it sounded like a

disease, his mouth turning even thinner. If he would just stop with the proto-scowl, it would do wonders for him.

Em suppressed another sigh. *Stick with one problem at a time.* "Okay. So what was the guy's name?"

"George. George Cavanaugh."

She grabbed a slice of scratch paper, digging in her purse for a pen. "And...what timeframe are we talking about? Give me a year he... The last year you saw him."

"According to your calendar?" He frowned slightly, his thin dark eyebrows coming together and his upper lip twitching a bit as if it wanted to curl. "Somewhere near 1760, *anno Domini*. Time moves... It is difficult."

"Cavanaugh—is that the way it's spelled? Okay, good. I'm going to see what I can dig up. You, uh, do you want, would you *like* to go through some of the books here?" A stray draft brought her a whiff of cardamom—she should maybe ask him about his cologne. It just made her hungry, though.

He hesitated. "I...am not averse to it."

"Would it make you happy?" God, it was like pulling teeth. Hadn't anyone ever asked him what he preferred before?

"Happy?" A small, tight smile touched his mouth. His shoulders hunched slightly. "What is that?"

"You know, rainbows, sunshine, the world not being a total drag? You have to remember the feeling." Another thought struck her. "Or did you always want to be a genie?"

"I was a slave." He tipped his head back, studied the fabled glass dome, a lens staring at billowing dark clouds. The rain had turned to sleet. "There was nothing to want."

This just keeps getting better. "My God, that's awful."

"It is the way of the world. Yes, I would find it pleasing to absorb as many of these books as I can." A long pause, while he studied the ceiling like it held a secret or two. "May I?"

She waved a hand. "Knock yourself out, you don't have to ask. If I find something—"

"Just say my name. I will hear."

"Hal. Okay. Go have fun, find me when you're done."

He didn't pop out of existence this time, thank God. He just got up, like a normal human being, and headed for the stairs. Maybe he would start at the top and work down, or maybe he had a secret genie reading list.

Em shook her head. Her hair was getting in her face. *God. This poor guy. No wonder he's weird.* She stared at the scrap of paper. *George Cavanaugh, 1760.*

What would it be like, to wake up after two and a half centuries plus and find out the whole world had changed? Or to be a slave—he'd said *bearers*, plural, which meant more than one person bossing him around; how long ago had he been enslaved? There was bound to be some emotional baggage on that. And those other "bearers"—he talked about them as if they were related. A whole happy family of assholes with a genie. They sounded egocentric as fuck-all.

And he went around calling *May* selfish. Okay, sometimes she was thoughtless, but she would never do something like make someone a *slave*. The "bearers" didn't sound very smart, either, which was probably a blessing. God only knew how much damage a smart sociopath could do with a genie.

Well, if there was one genie, maybe there had to be more? The stories didn't come from nowhere. Maybe, before looking into this Cavanaugh asshole, she should get a more solid idea of *Hal*. Just in the interests of figuring out how to get the damn ring off her finger and her life back to normal.

Em found she was rubbing the flat agate with her right middle finger, a thoughtful motion. The ring moved a little, and she stopped, staring at it.

It hadn't moved before.

She pulled it along her finger, testing. It slid to her

knuckle and got stuck—well, okay, maybe she was premen-
strual and swelling a bit. She slid it back, looked at the screen
in front of her.

Well, no time like the present. She settled herself, and
typed in *how do you get rid of a genie?*

28

OUR TITHES

SAINT BARTHOLOMEW'S CATHEDRAL LOOMED LARGE AND gray on Fortis Avenue. Though Peakes End was definitely older, the church looked flat-out eternal. The parsonage, tucked alongside the main bulk like a nest-edge propping up a stone wing, and Peter Cavanaugh almost shuddered as he edged along the mossy, crumbling concrete path between the outer wall and the church. He climbed the three steps and knocked politely. He would have to change when he got home; the rain was full of ice and he wasn't wearing a coat.

It would be dangerous to walk up to this particular door in anything that could hide a weapon.

"Yes?" Father Lantoreux, lean and dark-haired, opened it himself. Milky, rain-fogged sunlight struggled to reach the slippery steps, touched the priest's white collar and fell into his cassock without a murmur. His narrow eyes betrayed no shock or impatience at seeing a stranger on his doorstep, but then, a father would not.

The Papists, the old man would sometimes sneer. *Always so theatrical.*

What would happen, Peter wondered, if he yanked on the

hilt nestled at the small of his back and plunged the crystal-bladed dagger into the good Father's belly? It might even kill one of the fighting order of Saint Bartholomew. No, Peter wasn't wearing a coat, but a knife was so easy to hide.

You need that blade for other things. Instead, he proffered the manila envelope. The priest examined him, and invisible feathers brushed against Peter's hair.

"Sophic," the good father said quietly. "To what do I owe the honor?"

Well, that answered the question of whether the Bartholomews knew their asses from holes in the ground, in his late father's somewhat pungent phrasing. "We aren't enemies," Peter said, carefully. "Our brotherhood has come across some...disturbing information, and we offer it in the spirit of cooperation."

"And fish fly." The man's hand extended, though, and he took the envelope. "What is it you want in return? Since you are businessmen."

"We pay our tithes, Father." *All of them. And with interest, too.*

Father Lantoreux's nose was a wonder of Gallic architecture, and he wrinkled it a little. "God requires only faith."

In that case, he should come around more often. And bring booze. "Yours will no doubt equip you to face one of your old enemies." He shook his head slightly, searching for the right note of carelessness. "There's a witch in town, Father. This comes straight from the old man himself."

He turned and walked away, careful not to slip on the moss. The brothers of Saint Bartholomew's order trained all their lives to deal with a certain kind of nonhuman, invisible intelligence, one less useful than malevolent. Their regrettable vows about safeguarding the innocent were pretty flexible when it came to females, though, just like in every other century. Inside the envelope was a scrap of cheap carpet, brought back through space on the claws of one of the balked, almost-dead Appetites, and the terror soaking it would no doubt prove a lodestone to a brother tasked to find and destroy what they thought of as Satan's spawn.

His wingtips slipped; he almost went down in a heap. Still, Peter felt oddly cheerful.

It was really quite gratifying, the way the priest had gone pale.

❧ 29 ❧

STRANGE CONCEPTS

HAL REACHED THE LAW AND FINANCE SECTION BEFORE HE thinned out, oil soaking through a tortoise shell. The books welcomed him, and he spent a short while—after making certain he fully grasped the mechanics of their banking and the finer details of their financial structures—ascertaining the organization of the rest of the subjects. It was quite logical, though there was a distressing dearth of what Cavanaugh would have called natural philosophy or useful occultia. Of course, such things would not be in a *public* library. The Fratres—and their predecessors—had always been very clear that the hidden powers were only to be accessed by responsible property-owners.

The great explosion of printed matter, however, had come about in fiction. Sometime during his long dormancy, the novel as a form had reached heights of popularity undreamed of by the men of culture in Cavanaugh's time.

The knowledge contained in their other books—especially history—would be useful, but Hal found himself pulled toward the vast glittering field of imagination. He thinned out even further, first sweeping through the children's section to gain a basic understanding, then turning his attention to the fiction shelves.

Such worlds they imagined! *Clarissa* was nothing to this, though he could remember Cavanaugh and his brothers denouncing it as a piece of sentimental trash. Women wrote novels now, though, as well as scholarly works. There seemed little women could *not* do in this new world. Their voices were marvelous—entirely new horizons, the other half of humanity no longer locked in the silence of the ignored. They wore what they pleased and even owned property.

Simply amazing. Wonderful. Surely they would reach the stars, now that they were not wasting themselves on petty differences?

As soon as it was born, that hope was crushed. Some of the novels were full of dark things, indeed.

Oh, that's why she...interesting. Now, what is that?

An entire section labeled *Romance*. Chivalry and knights? Did they still dream of such things—eras so bygone the stink of their sweat and feces was forgotten, and only the rosewater and spectacle remained?

Hal intended to only brush the surface of the Romance section. Instead, he almost solidified in shock, halfway through a bookcase. *Oh. That...that was unexpected.*

A few more moments showed him just how valuable these books were. They were not only full of the changing mores of this society, but also of that most winning of creatures: *women*. Their dreams, their wishes, their desires, their secrets. What a marvelous gift they had given to males, mortal or otherwise, in writing so plainly what they longed for, how they chose their mates.

Hal solidified just enough to see who came into these aisles, searching for answers.

Now *that* was strange. Three women were in this one

aisle, conversing in low tones about authors, heroes, and "happy-ever-afters." They were all three vivid with interest, though two were young and one was, by the state of her hips, a well-married matron.

Did the mortal men...not read these? Incomprehensible stupidity on their part.

The science, the technology—he had a basic but thorough grasp, and it would be refined as he studied the world around him. *This* treasure trove deserved his attention now. He could barely believe his luck.

Hidden in these books might be the key to keeping his bearer....happy. The more he could refine his handling of her, the better chance he stood of at least convincing her of his usefulness.

Why do I care? One mortal is just like another.

Except *she* was not. In all the years, of all the bearers, not one had even thought to ask of his freedom, or his own desires. Perhaps, had the ring fallen into the hands of a woman before now...but that was beside the point. He was here, now, with *this* woman, and he craved to remain so.

"...paranormal romance," one of the younger women said. "I eat that up with a *spoon*."

"I can never get over the shifter ones," the matron replied. "I start thinking about the mass conversion from human to honey badger. It just yanks me right out of the story."

"Physics, the great downfall of every love story," the third woman chimed in. They laughed, a sound soft and pleasant as the rustle of dove's wings, and Hal thinned out again to encompass the entire section. He set himself to absorbing them *all*, and congratulated himself that soon, very soon, he would understand more about his maddening, fascinating bearer.

For a long while he soaked into them, slipping from book

to book with growing confidence. The men in these books represented an ideal, to be sure, but it was a fairly steady one. Even a mortal man could understand the basics—fidelity above all, a form of chivalry, competence, and an admission that a woman was the most amazing creature ever created. There were "historical" books—some full of glaring inaccuracy, others obviously carefully researched—and a breathtaking kaleidoscope of male "types", from the domineering protector to the gentler man driven to revenge or protection. "Faith-based" romances, full of Papist pap, Protestant self-denial, and quite a few "humbled" heroes—and the "paranormal" ones. Some of the latter had obviously dug into troves of arcane knowledge by the shovelful. Was this the only way they could compass the strangeness of invisible powers?

It beggared belief. But now he could explain much in terms his bearer would understand. Did she read these books? Which of the mortal heroes were her favorites? What did she long for, dream of?

He was pulled sideways into the "science" fiction next, a strange section amalgamated with what they called "fantasy." Unfamiliar concepts forced their way into his receptive consciousness, and it would take time to digest such a mass of information. A mortal man would die of old age before he could absorb even a tenth of what this building held.

It was *glorious*.

Little by little, a strange sensation crept through him. Almost a chill. At first he paid little heed, but it sharpened into an unease. He slid through the nonfiction section once more, absorbing what he could in another vast lump, before coalescing at the railing of the second floor, looking down into the vast central well of the library. The computers were near the back, set into rows of cabinets, and they had become crowded.

He looked for his bearer's curly dark head and could not find it. Frowning, Hal thinned out into insubstantiality again, searching for his fetter. The chill sharpened yet again, and he sensed danger.

She had left the building.

🙚 30 🙘

TRUST YOURSELF

EM LEANED AGAINST THE PRINTER, TRYING TO IGNORE THE shelves of impulse candy near the long package-wrapping counter. Emailing everything she'd found to herself and heading out to find a cheaper—and faster—way to print it was the most efficient way to tackle the situation, especially since there was a CopySend two blocks away. The library's printers meant well, but they were lumbering beasts and she didn't have cash in her wallet for the copy fees. Two blocks away, she could sign in, send it to a lightning-fast machine, and use her debit card.

The urge to sign onto her bank statements was well-nigh overpowering, but she resisted it mightily.

She was fairly sure she'd found the guy—George Alfred Cavanaugh, one of the leading luminaries of something called the Sophic Gentlemen's Club. The Club seemed to be a rival organization to the Freemasons—at least, there was a lot of back-and-forthing in some old newspapers. Some guy in England, bless his strange little historical fetishes, had scanned a bunch of pamphlets dealing with a sort of war between Freemasons and the Sophics—or the Fratres, as they liked to call themselves. There were accusations of all sorts of nifty stuff—double-dealing, ungentlemanly fisticuffs, and hints of "offenses against God and man." Which, given the 1700s, could have been anything from sodomy to an interest in vaccination.

The war had seemed mostly confined to insults in various newsletters and tongue-in-cheek adverts, but there were hints of something else—a number of starchy English "authorities" had printed notices about disturbing the peace and altercations in "clubs." Probably not nightclubs, either. This Cavanaugh guy seemed pretty high up in the Sophics.

It was enough to make her wonder if the Freemasons really were a cabal secretly running the world instead of just old guys who couldn't decide what kind of gravy they wanted. Working for a caterer part time in college had gotten her into one of their lodges, and she remembered the boss running her capable hands back through her long, curling, gray hair and swearing under her breath because the clients wouldn't specify *white* or *brown* gravy without arguing over it for a week, for God's sake.

It wasn't exactly the image of a brotherhood that could control powerful wish-granting hunks. Or maybe it was, and that was why the world hadn't ended.

Emily even had a few moments, looking through a website on 18th-century "grimoires"—some type of magic book, apparently—of thinking maybe Hal could teach her a little bit about real magic. The idea that it was all true, that she could maybe learn to do some of the shit people only saw in movies, was powerfully attractive.

Then it occurred to her, well, maybe she was better off not knowing, especially if it had to do with enslaving people. It didn't sound like a happy time all around.

The orange nylon carpet in here looked like it was from the seventies, and was worn down to the nap in more than one place. *God. I need a sandwich.* Better yet, a burger, dripping with cheese and bacon. And pickles. There was that place—was it on Fifteenth?—that served milkshakes, too. A peanut-butter-Oreo milkshake. They would put bacon in, if you asked. May had talked her into it, and it was a glorious taste sensation but not one you could indulge in more than once a year.

She is thoughtless and selfish.

He didn't know a damn thing about May. He didn't know about her growing up in that fundamentalist shithole of a town, or the fact that she regularly volunteered at a no-kill shelter out in Gole Heights. He didn't know about May coming over almost every night for a few months after the divorce, with a movie or a magazine or something in a casserole dish, knowing that the last thing Em wanted to do was cook or think about what had just happened. During finals crunch week, it was always May making sure their mini-fridge had the healthiest snacks they could dredge up as they starved through college. There was May when Em had pneumonia that bad, scary winter, driving her to the hospital and sitting for three hours holding Em's hand as she coughed and choked and shivered with fever. It was May who comforted Em each time she called her parents and heard her mother's disappointment, her father's silent wishing she'd been born a boy, May who was listed as beneficiary on Em's 401(k) if something happened.

Now there was a thought. Had the genie touched her retirement fund? She was going to have to seriously think about the implications of the whole damn financial thing.

The printer shuddered, spitting out sheet after sheet. She'd have to get something to eat and try to find the gigantic whipped-cream house again. Would the address be in her GPS as "home"? Maybe Hal had been that thorough. Who knew? Hopefully he was enjoying the library.

Em told the persistent sense that she hadn't logged out of her email to go away. She'd checked four times before standing up from her chair and stretching, and another two times before she picked up her purse, and walked back *twice* to make sure before she left the building.

It paid to be sure. Especially when you'd just been chucked into the deep end of, well, *magic*. She scratched her chin thoughtfully on her blue scarf, relishing its familiar comfort.

Did the kid behind the counter, doing something at a large paper-cutting machine, know about this? Did anyone outside, on the sidewalk, going about their daily lives, know? How about government people? Police, EMTs, first responders? Did the military know? Were there secret wars going on with genies and other, darker things? Things like the big hairy whatevers in her apartment?

Appetites, Hal called them. Like bloodhounds, except they bring the prey back once it is dead.

Ugh. Her phone buzzed. She dug it out, wondering if she should check to see if, say, Becky's number was still in her contacts. Or Brett's email.

It was an 800 number. Telemarketer, probably. Even a genie couldn't stop robocalls.

God. Would anyone she'd met at work recognize her? So many questions, ramifications, her head hurt trying to wrap around it all.

The printer finally finished. She winced a little as she saw the end total, but it was about half of what it would be at the library, and quicker, too. Her receipt spat out of a slit on the machine's front, and she spent a few moments tidying the stack of freshly printed paper. Somewhere in it might be a clue. After a while, she'd just dumped everything about Cavanaugh into a cloud document and—

Wait, did I sign out of that? Well, of course she had—it was attached to her email suite.

She was getting silly. Lunch was *definitely* called for. It would be more like dinner by the time she actually got a table somewhere. She had a spot, so she might as well stay parked —and pay the exorbitant rates—unless she wanted a drive-thru and the concomitant worry of navigating the beginning of rush hour. Even a genie might not be able to deal with the traffic on the freeway around five PM.

Em glanced at the print shop's windows. A chill slid down her back, along her arms, through the backs of her legs.

It was too dark—well, the clouds of sleet overhead were heavy, and it was winter. The streetlamps were blinking and stuttering as they woke up, though the cars hadn't turned their headlights on yet. People hurried under the ice-spattering deluge, so Em took a few moments to stuff the thick sheaf of maybe-useless paper into the laptop pocket in her purse. It would be heavy, and hell on her shoulders, but that would keep them from getting soaked.

Sleet splatted dully against the window; the wind was up, too. It looked *damn* cold out there.

And take, for example, the guy standing by the newspaper boxes right outside the CopySend's automatic door. He had a long dark coat with a high collar, but it looked far too thin for this weather. His hat was weird, too—a wide brim and a round crown, reminding her vaguely of old Westerns. He just stood there, facing the street, and ice-freighted rain ran in long strings off his hat brim.

Why did that bother her so much? Maybe he was waiting for a bus? But the nearest stop was in the middle of the next block, or in front of the library two blocks away in the other direction. If he wanted a newspaper, why didn't he just go around the front of the boxes and get one? Was he watching the office building across the street, or the sandwich shop on their first floor?

Emily's stomach gave an unhappy burble.

May had texted her. *Planning the Xmas party with Gloria. You game?*

Not really. She could wait until she was less cranky to reply, though. Maybe she could even tactfully bow out this year. Or get the genie to hang some tinsel. That was, if she hadn't figured out how to get rid of him in two months.

He hadn't shown up yet. Maybe he was reading up on a couple hundred years of history. Explaining Thanksgiving and indigenous genocide to him was going to be a chore.

Em stopped just outside the range of the automatic door. What was bothering her so much? It wasn't her phone, or her slight irritation at being asked to do the scut work of organizing for yet another Christmas party she probably wouldn't attend for more than a couple hours, if that. It wasn't even that she was so hungry she could probably put away a cheeseburger and a half before she slowed down.

It was her feet. They refused to budge, planted against ancient, cheap, tough-as-nails, industrial carpeting. Her very sensible rainproof boots—fished out of a coat closet in the front hall of the whipped-cream house—just wouldn't move.

That's your instinct right there, May would say. *Trust it. Trust yourself.*

And oh, how Em had needed to hear that, especially after Steven. Endlessly agonizing over whether or not she was doing the right thing.

You know you did.

Just like she knew, right now, that something was very, very wrong, and she needed to stay still.

Her gaze snagged, again, on the man in the black hat. Where had she seen a hat like that before? And he was really,

really damp. What was he doing just *standing* there? It was weird, but not dangerous, right?

He moved, restlessly, as if sensing her notice. His hat made funny little bobbing motions, like he was coughing. He turned, and she caught a flash of white high on his collar. A priest? The closest church was...well, goddamn, she didn't know. Not within three blocks.

Still, it was the city, and you saw all sorts of stuff on the sidewalk.

The maybe-priest took a few long swinging strides; Em watched as he glided across the plate-glass window. A FedEx truck barreled to a stop, throwing up a sheet of rainwater, and the lone CopyStop employee scuttled past Em to help the driver, a harried-looking strawberry-blond man who hadn't got the memo about winter and was wearing navy-blue shorts. Just looking at him made Em feel a little cold.

"You need an umbrella, ma'am?" the CopyStop kid asked her, craning over his shoulder while he carried a stack of boxes into the brightly lit haven of his little store.

"No," she heard herself say, and tested her legs. They moved just fine now. "Thanks anyway, though."

She braced herself and hurried out into the curtains of icy, stinging sleet, turning away from the direction the maybe-priest had gone. It would mean crossing the street upstream instead of down to get back to her car, but that was probably for the best.

Screw getting a restaurant meal. She wanted to be home, posthaste, even if it meant sitting in some traffic. And even if it wasn't really home, but a white creampuff of a house too big for any reasonable human being.

❧ 31 ❧

WHAT FEAR IS

SHE WAS IN ONE OF THE SMALL METAL CAGES THEY USED TO lift themselves from floor to floor. Hal, deciding it probably was not quite wise to surprise her by coalescing in such cramped quarters, waited on the floor she'd parked on. The bell to announce the lift's presence dinged, and when the door opened, he was surprised to see her soaked almost all the way through, shivering, and very pale. Her curling hair hung in wet ribbons, and she had just sneezed, her hand cupped over her nose. Those wide dark forest-eyes met his, and Hal, possessing a stomach since he was corporeal, wondered why said internal organ suddenly dropped inside him.

Well, what would one of those chivalric heroes do? Take off his jacket and offer it to her, of course. But he could do so much more.

"Oh, hey." She lowered her hand, wrinkling her nose. Even her knitted scarf was soaked. "Got all your reading done?"

"You left the library." He tried not to glower, stepping forward as she shuffled out of the lift. It chimed and prepared itself for another trip.

"Yeah, I had to go print some stuff out." Her boots squeaked a little, they were so damp. "There was a strange guy—"

The power leapt to obey him. She gasped, water leaving her hair and clothing in long ribbons, drawn free without heat so as not to scald her. Then, very carefully, the warmth—just a few degrees, so she stopped shivering. She looked a little less pale now. Much better.

"There." He watched her expression change from shock to pleasure, and congratulated himself. "A strange man, you say?" The chill of danger had not receded, but there was no reason to make *her* feel it. Had she been menaced by a mortal?

"Yeah. It's the weirdest thing." She hitched her bag higher on her slim shoulder. "Crap. I can never remember where I park in these things."

"Over here." He pointed, tried to decide whether carrying her bag was the romantic thing to do. Or an arm over her shoulder? No, that was too much. If this were one of the novels, how would the hero behave? Courteously, of course. At least she was dry, and no longer freezing.

"You're a lifesaver. Anyway, yeah. Guy was just standing out in the rain. Who knows, though, in the city you see all sorts of—"

He *moved*, pushing her behind the nearest round concrete pillar before he was quite aware of the projectiles flashing her way. They were very fast, and he stepped *aside* for a moment to consider them. Ugly things—yes, he had absorbed the knowledge of *bullets*. The arquebuses and muskets of Cavanaugh's day had evolved considerably.

In the end, though, they were simply mortal missiles. Even if a faint scrim of not-quite-light danced on the blunt nose of each one.

Ah. A newer magic, and one he had considerable experience of. The Church, it seemed, was alive and well. Not to mention still dabbling in things its public face professed horror of and disbelief in.

Hal spread his fingers, and the bullets ceased struggling against his grasp on the timeflow. When he rejoined its stream, they would drop to the ground, harmless, chattering and hissing as the magical charge on them fizzed uselessly. The next item, of course, was their source, and Hal found himself, for the first time in centuries, facing a fighting priest of the Order of Saint Bartholomew.

A lean, blond, blue-eyed young man in a round-crowned hat, wet clear through from the rain outside like Hal's bearer had been. The priest held a pistol in one hand, obviously meaning to injure or even kill Hal's bearer, and his other hand clasped the hilt of a straight sword with a tar-black blade.

How interesting. He had never seen such a weapon, and probed at it deftly with nonphsyical fingers. It did not fight his hold on this small sliver of the timestream, nor did it resonate when plucked at. Clearly *this* was what the priest meant to use on Hal. Caution was called for.

Time dropped back into place, and Hal's foot flicked out, connecting solidly with the mortal priest's midsection. The man went flying and his pistol barked wildly, scattering bullets in a wide arc. None of them approached Hal's bearer, so he blurred forward, leaping lightly atop one of the concrete teeth meant to stop a metal chariot from plowing through the lifts. The priest landed with a snap of breaking bones and the crunch of crumpling metal, sliding down the side of a large black vehicle parked on the dividing line between two spots.

In Cavanaugh's day, the coachman who did something similar would earn a curse at best, and a brawl at worst.

The mortal was chanting in Latin, between ragged gasps. "*In nomine Patris—*"

"*Et filii, et Spiritus Sancti.*" Hal joined the litany. "But you are not facing one of your usual enemies, priest."

The mortal's wet, clean-shaven face, speckled with blood—he coughed, spitting more claret—contorted. "*Diabolus,*" he hissed, pushing himself upward. It was amazing, to see how so fragile and shattered an organism could force itself to move. His hat had been knocked away, and without it, he looked even younger.

Hal shook his head. "No, my friend. Your god has no quarrel with me."

The priest raised his gun; Hal stepped sideways to place himself before the barrel's small, angry mouth. There was a deathly silence behind him—his bearer had not been harmed. He would *know*, and in any case, the pillar he had placed her behind was quite capable of deflecting—

Hal realized his mistake just as the mortal lunged. Perhaps it was desperation that gave him such speed, or his god. In any case, he rammed the black-bladed sword through Hal's chest.

Pain, faint and faraway behind a queer draining sensation.

How interesting. His hand flashed out, caught the mortal with a short, sharp cracking sound, and the priest went flying again.

Normally he would simply step sideways into the incorporeal, but the blade was a black, rusted nail holding him to physicality. Hal grasped the swordhilt, pulling it free inch by inch. One of his knees buckled. *Ah, I see. The Church has loosened its restrictions on the older ceremonial sorceries.* The blade stung his fingers when he sought to clasp it instead of the hilt, which was rapidly becoming awkward. His arms simply weren't long enough. "Ah." From very far away, he heard his own voice, baffled and somewhat hoarse.

"Hal?" It was Emily, right next to him. "Oh, my God, *Hal!*"

He motioned at the sword. She let out a sobbing breath,

both hands clasped to her mouth, her hair gloriously mussed and her eyes wide as saucers.

She was concerned. Fearful. For *him*.

He motioned again at the swordhilt and grabbed what he could of the blade, ignoring the fresh pain through his palms. He pulled, and there was very little time. The priest was somewhere to his right, near the lift, and possibly still had his pistol. Emily was vulnerable, and Hal could not *move*.

So this is what fear is. The thought was very slow, and now he saw the true power of the blade. All it had to do was hold him for long enough, and the priest would attack his defenseless mortal bearer; a bullet to her heart or head would send Hal back to the castle in a rage of...

Emily grabbed the swordhilt. It was wrong, her beautiful hands should not have to touch such a thing. Her mouth moved slightly. She was repeating *Hal*, over and over again. It was a fine time to wish he had a true name, one he could give her, hear her lips shape.

She pulled, squeezing her eyes shut, and the sword eased free of his chest just as the priest, slow as a damaged engine but just as powerfully determined, lifted his head from the shapeless heap he had become near the lift doors. Sound, color, breath all roared back into Hal, and he heard Em's sobbing breath and her "My *God,* a man with a sword, what the *fuck*—"

She let go of the hilt as if it burned her, too, and the sword hit concrete with a loud metallic clatter. The priest lifted his remaining weapon, and Em's head snapped to the side. She saw the pistol rising, and her mouth opened as if to cry warning.

The rushing of power filled Hal's ears, and he *moved.*

NEAT TRICK

"STAY STILL." EM SWALLOWED, HARD. HER STOMACH WAS *still* unhappy with the whole blinking-from-the-parking-garage-to-home thing. It was a good thing she *hadn't* eaten lunch. "Oh, Jesus. We should really get you to a hospital."

The genie was *bleeding*, thick trickles of wrong-looking dark red fluid about the consistency of glue. The hole went right through him, and she sloshed peroxide over a wad of cotton balls. The whipped-cream house had a white-and-gold bathroom right next to her bedroom, and along with her usual clutter under the sink was a first-aid kit she *definitely* didn't remember buying. It had just sort of...appeared, while she was digging frantically for the cotton balls.

Gauze. She needed gauze, for God's sake.

"I will be well enough." He winced, looking down at his chest with detached interest. His shoulders were absurdly broad, and with the blue sweater off he looked...well, if there hadn't been the two big bleeding wounds on him, she might have had a few moments of artistic appreciation of that torso. Maybe the sweater had been like genie Spanx, hiding him.

His arms were pretty respectable, too; she could have sworn he'd been much leaner before.

"This might hurt." She bit her lip and pressed the wad of cotton and disinfectant to his chest. "Did it nick your spine? Jesus. Seriously, this needs medical attention, and *right now*." The lights over the mirror were shaped like lilies, and gave out a warm golden glow. There were two bathtubs—a cast iron one she'd seen in a *Restoration Hardware* catalog and a sunken one she didn't ever remember coming across. Who needed two goddamn bathtubs?

It was *insane*. Everything about this was.

"I am not mortal." Hal winced, lifting his hands. His ponytail had loosened a bit, and without his hair scraped so severely back he looked a little younger. A little softer, too. "You do not need to—"

"The *hell* I don't!" What was *with* him? He was acting like...like...she couldn't even find a word for it. "You just got stabbed with a *sword!* By that guy outside the CopySend, I might add."

"He was the strange man you saw?" His hand closed gently over hers. Very warm, very solid, and not shaking in the slightest. "He followed you, then. You should not have left the library."

You will not blame this on me, goddammit. "Excuse me? I am an *adult*, I can go where I damn well please. Do not try to derail this conversation. You got *stabbed*."

"It is already closing. Look." He peeled her fingers away, and the stained cotton balls gave her another burst of that queasy feeling.

The edges of the stab wound, flushed and raw, were sealing up, slowly but surely. The blood, except where the peroxide had touched it, was helping. It welled thick and gleaming, then somehow faded to skin color as the hole in the genie shrank.

"You're going to need a bandage." Her voice shook. This was worse than the car accident and Steven's bloody nose. "Two bandages." *I should have gauze on hand. I really should.*

"Emily." He plucked the sloppy wad of cotton and too-red genie blood from her, closed it in his free hand. When he opened his fingers, no trace remained. "Thank you."

"For what? That's a nice... We have to at least disinfect it, you could get..." Did genies get infections? Could she just smear some antibiotic ointment on it and call it good? Jesus.

He squeezed her fingers, gently. "All is well." He was trying to sound reassuring, she realized. "In an hour or less, I will be fully healed. That particular weapon is unpleasant, but I am on my guard now."

"Well, fantastic. That's just great." She tried to pull her hand away, but his fingers clamped down. Not painfully, just very decisively. "He could have *shot* you!"

"He certainly tried."

Thanks, that's ever so helpful. "Why?"

"He is a priest. Almost certainly of the Order of St. Bartholomew. He perhaps thinks me a demon. It is very interesting."

"Fascinating, I'm sure." Em tugged again, but he wouldn't let go. "First werewolves and now this."

"They were not ever human; they are Appetites, not were-wolves." He shook his head a little, winced again. The wound was making a very small, very definite sucking noise as it healed. It was so quiet in here, other than the two of them, that she could hear it. And her own breathing, and his. Plus the ragged stamp of her heartbeat in her ears. "And this priest was no doubt sent by the Fratres. Normally, they do not engage the help of the Church."

So there are actual werewolves. Good to know. "My mother is a Catholic." As if it mattered. "Look, you...I... He *shot* at you—"

"At you, actually."

Oh boy. She swayed a bit, and the peroxide bottle in her other hand sloshed. "Why...why would..."

"They think almost anything...abnormal...is witchery. In the old days, people were more pragmatic." He exhaled, a long pained breath. "The Fratres will have much explaining to do to our friend."

"Well, he's probably dead. He looked like he had a bunch of broken bones, and—" It hit her all at once. Good *God.* A priest. A *human being.*

Dead. Someone was maybe *dead.*

"Their god gives them certain dispensations. Priests of his kind are durable, for mortals." He shifted his shoulders to ease his back, and Em shook her head. This surgically clean, luxurious bathroom was nice, sure, but she really, *really* wanted her apartment with the familiar, persistent stains in the grout and the fact that she could reach for anything without looking, knowing exactly where everything was.

"You got stabbed." *I'm repeating myself.* "Someone *shot* at us. And whatever those hairy things were, you know what? It doesn't matter. I didn't sign up for this." Finally, she worked her wrist free of his grasp, even though he probably could have kept it. "I suppose it doesn't matter. I'm *in* it. Goddammit. Someone's dead. There's been a murder, and I'm an accessory."

"No. He is still alive."

Well, thank goodness for that. "How do you—no, wait, don't answer that." She shook her head vigorously, her hair whipping back and forth. One of her curls almost ended up in her mouth. "No way, no day."

"Emily—"

Well, at least he wasn't calling her *mistress* anymore. Yay. "*You* are going to sit right there and get bandaged." She glared at him, wishing her head didn't feel so funny and light. "Then we are going to get some dinner, and we can go through everything I found at the library today, and we're going to discuss just exactly how to get you free of this thing." *And everything back to the way it was.*

Hal's face settled back into severe somberness, but his gaze was uncomfortably direct. "You assume I *wish* to be free of it."

Well, yes. Yes she did. Wouldn't anyone? "Well, don't you? You said you're a slave."

"I was." He gazed at her, dark eyes dancing-alive. Had his face changed a little, too? The nose a little shorter, the cheekbones a little muted? A genie could probably look like whatever he wanted.

"So, do you want to be free, or do you just want me to give the ring to someone else? Someone who knows about all this stuff?"

"No, Emily." He spread the hand that had held hers against the glaring wound, and his eyelids dropped to half-mast. When he pulled his fingers away, there was nothing but a short, livid scar. Just like Dad's bypass surgery. "I do not wish another bearer."

"Oh." She swayed again, the peroxide almost falling from her slackening hand. "That's a pretty neat trick."

"Nobody has ever insisted on bandaging me before." His mouth turned up at one corner, slightly.

Em set the bottle down on the marble countertop next to the shell-shaped sink. "Yeah, well, your former, uh, bearers, were dicks."

With that, she blundered out of the bathroom, almost barking her shoulder on the doorway, and set off to find the kitchen again. This place was a pile, and she couldn't even imagine *living* here. It was only slightly better than a hotel, because all her stuff was here.

Halfway down the hall she stopped, feeling blindly for the

wall. A slightly bluish white paint made the corridor light and airy, and it certainly smelled better than the apartment building's public spaces. She had to lean against the wall, heavily, as her head swam. There were limits to what a girl could handle, for God's sake.

At you, actually.

Shot at. She'd been *shot* at, and could still hear the huge booming, feel the lurch of the world around her that was Hal just blinking into being next to her, then somehow she was behind a concrete pillar and hearing the zing-pop of bullets. It was nothing like it was on television or in the movies. In real life it was just loud and terrifying, and it made you want to pee because your entire body was too heavy and you couldn't run without dropping some ballast.

At least she hadn't pissed herself. There was that to be grateful for. Maybe.

It had all happened so *fast*. Peering around the pillar and seeing Hal, the point of the strange sword sticking out his back and dripping with that thick red gel, and coming face to face with her own cowardice—because she knew the right thing to do was to run out and help him, but she had frozen.

All her life she'd been the one to play it safe. Where had *that* gotten her? Still, it was probably too late to change.

So she pushed away from the wall, set her shoulders, and found herself twisting the ring on her finger, back and forth, meditatively.

It moved easily.

❧ 33 ❧

RENDERING UNTO

THE OLD MAN PACED. TO THE WINDOW, AND BACK. TO THE study window again, once more back to the desk. Outside, sleet slapped down in waves, beating on soggy grass and a few stray leaves blown in on a restless, chill wind. Slow, measured footsteps. Every time he stopped at the desk, he glanced at the map, which still stubbornly refused to show any more than it had the last fifty times he'd checked it.

"It's taking too long," he muttered, sometimes softly, sometimes a little louder, as if daring Peter to disagree.

That was a dare Peter did not take. Instead, he focused on the newspaper. The obituaries were a sad crop—looked like Eldridge Moss was being called "a loving father" and "pillar of the community." Repressing a snort at this marvelous but completely necessary misstatement, he glanced over the paper's rim, enjoying the flickering warmth of the fireplace. "Perhaps the brothers of Bartholomew have grown cautious."

"Levity is unhelpful." Thin lips lifted in a snarl, and the nose-bulb twitched in time to the syllables.

Yes, indeed, the old man was in a mood.

"I was not attempting it, sir." The lie came smoothly. "I was merely remarking that the Church has to keep certain things below the sightline. As do we." The leather-clad books in this room made small creaking sounds, responding to the charged atmosphere. The old man was throwing off concentrated waves of frustration and impatience. Powerful fuel, but unreliable.

"At least the spirit will disappear when the thief is dead." A baleful glare directed at the window, as if the old man suspected the ring's current owner—who, to be fair, probably had no fucking idea what she'd picked up, and probably didn't even *use* the damn thing—to be standing out on the sodden lawn. "That will convince them of the Devil."

And what if the priest takes the ring? But that was unlikely—they did not strip the bodies of their victims anymore. They preferred to go after targets with moderate estates, and add *those* to church holdings; the corpse was left for the authorities to fold into their statistics for the year, rendering unto Caesar the problem of where to bury those who dabbled with the wrong sort of powers according to Rome. It would be a simple matter to retrieve the ring from police impound.

Once the creature was removed from play and the map cleared up, nothing would be easier.

The hilt pressing against Peter's spine was still comforting, but also painful. He didn't dare alter his posture. He slept clutching the knife under his pillow, and just this morning he had taken the whole thing, sheath and all, into the shower with him as well.

You couldn't be too careful. When the map changed, the old man would be distracted, and Peter would rid the world of a monster. Then, his reward would be waiting to slip onto his finger. Nice and easy.

It was a plan even the old man might have liked.

Peter settled further into his the chair and listened to the footsteps. Back, a pause, and forth. The fire popped and crackled, and he wished the old man would take a bath or something. His ancient scrawny frame was rank as a goat's, and it made the whole room smell.

❧ 34 ❧

LOST IN HELL'S HOLLOW

HAL'S CHEST ACHED. IT HAD BEEN A LONG TIME SINCE HE had met a weapon that could wound him, that was indeed half the pain.

The other half...well.

Em sat on the hardwood floor, priceless Persian rugs spreading their jewel tones around her. She'd pushed the exquisite curve of the coffee table away and settled her back against the pale leather couch. Drawing up one knee, she scanned a piece of paper, set it carefully in one of the piles arranged on the floor before her. She'd tried to confine her hair in a braid, but curls worked free every time she forgot and tried to run her hands back through it, in frustration or fascination. She absorbed much more slowly than he did, but she wanted to sort through the papers first, and he found he did not mind. While she read, he could watch her, and that was...satisfying.

She had insisted on his partaking of dinner with her—the large dining room was too much, so it was the breakfast bar in her lovely new kitchen with its blond wood cabinets and the Corian countertops, artificial stone in many colors. The food, delivered by a cheerful young man in a metal chariot who had thanked her kindly for a gratuity, was still hot. *Indian*, she called it, the trammeled empire now free, and the explosion of tastes and textures was quite novel indeed. Hal did not eat for fuel, but it was pleasant to consume, and even more pleasant to watch her sate mortal hunger.

Sometimes she played with the ring while she read, and each time his breath would threaten to stop. She appeared not to notice the ease with which it slid upon her finger, instead of being fused to her flesh. If he could have held her hand just a little bit longer, he might have thought to seal it to her, and his almost-disobedience might well have gone unnoticed for some while.

"Here's something," she said, finally, holding up two closely-printed sheets and tucking her pencil behind her ear. It almost vanished into her hair. "Give this an eyeball, see what you think."

She was certainly systematic. The piles were: definitely useless, probably useless, interesting but off-topic, possibly useful, and useful. The "useful" pile was short indeed.

Occasionally, she asked him a question. Could she wish for her old apartment back? Indeed, but if the Appetites had found her there once, it might not be safe. Had any of the other bearers taken the ring off willingly? They generally died of violence after sending him away. Why the hell would they send him away? If they desired privacy—for example, while wenching, or—

Wenching? Her eyebrow had lifted, and he could only shrug helplessly.

She'd asked him if the wound hurt. It was mending, he would be more prepared in the future. How many attacks did he expect? It was difficult to say. Was her home address changed in her phone? She'd looked at the device and frowned. *Huh. Look at that, it is.* How much money did she have? As much as she wanted, money was easy. She had tapped at her small device again and let out a small sound of shock, before gulping and setting the damn thing aside.

He hoped the amount was adequate.

Hal leaned forward, took the papers. He had decided not to stand, looming over her; he had also decided to remake his appearance slightly, after the illustrations on the covers of those fascinating romance books. He quite liked the solidity of this form, and had remade the blue sweater somewhat to accommodate its different proportions. She seemed easier with him when he copied her posture.

Now, in a battered pair of loose knit pants with penguins dotted over the fabric and a sweatshirt much too large for her, his bearer waited while he scanned the pages.

"The London Evening Post," she said. "1763. Cavanaugh's name is in the second column, about halfway down."

A CERTAIN *CAVANAUGHE, of BLESTON PLACE, would advertise for the Return of a Finger, lost in HELL'S HOLLOW, this Sunday last, no Doubt while on his Way to Church.*

"I see it," he murmured, absorbing the information. "And yes, Bleston Place. Quite a scandalous little event, to be stated so. But he was a very rich man, and that made for interest in his case."

She nodded, thoughtfully. "Reading between the lines, I think—I'm not really sure, but I *think* it's saying he was attacked and someone cut his finger off?"

"Hm." His eyebrows drew together. "That's interesting. I would not have...ah."

"What?" All her attention was focused on him. She leaned forward, and being the sole object of her regard was... pleasant.

Very pleasant.

"It might imply that in a fit of drunkenness, he cut his

own finger off." A small but distinct possibility. Wine did much to a man.

"Jesus. Was he trying to get rid of the ring?" Her tiny shudder was gratifying. If he could lead her to believe only such a thing would free her of Hal—but that would be dangerous. He suspected this mortal woman possessed the unflinching resolve to do such a thing, were it to be necessary. She did not know the half of her strength.

So, a judicious retreat was called for. "Unlikely. He rather enjoyed wielding me. He did have a habit of deep religiosity while sotted, though." Hal considered this. "We know his finger was removed. How, though...ah."

"What?"

"There were several among the Fratres who might have used his debauches to attack him." Perhaps one of them—Islington, Breeks, Lord Reacher—had merely waited for such an occasion? Or perhaps, in a fit during one of his black moods and well into his cups, Cavanaugh had been overwhelmed with religious sentiment—or simple fear? "Still...he had something as close to immortality as I can grant. It is unlikely the loss of a phalange would have killed him."

"Well, that's all nightmare fuel, thanks." She stretched a little, arching her back, and Hal dropped his gaze back to the paper. "There's something else—there was an auction of all his stuff in 1764. That's on the second page."

He nodded, slowly. Lord Reacher, of course, would have been the one to arrange that. Of all the Fratres, he was the one who envied common-born Cavanaugh the most, and without Hal's fetter, certain revenges would no doubt have been indulged in. "Yet the man arranging that could not have been unaware of the ring."

"So somehow he chopped his finger off and...what, someone picked it up with the ring attached, and ran away?"

"Not entirely out of the question. He may even have been

attacked by a husband or pimp of the women he was set to enjoy that evening."

Disgust on her transparent face. Her eyes darkened. "He sounds like a real winner. So someone chops his finger off, and the ring gets...pawned, maybe?"

"That could happen." It was, indeed, fairly likely. "Normally, he was exceeding cautious. That night, though, he wished to celebrate, and did not..." *Did not wish to force me to see or partake, for once.*

"Maybe someone was just waiting for when you weren't around." A delicate shudder raced through her; she glanced at the rest of the stack of paper waiting for her. "Well, at least we're making progress."

Of a sort. "Was there a funeral announcement?"

"Not that I found. Just the auction. But we *are* talking about two and a half centuries ago. It's amazing I found this."

A blast of sound broke the quiet and she reached for her tiny phone with an elegant motion. She was so unconsciously graceful; how had he not noticed the exact curve of her fragile wrist, the line of her cheekbone, the shapeliness of her throat before?

"Hullo, my dear." A new, richer timbre to her voice. "What's on fire?"

Gabbling from the instrument. Who was it?

"Yes, I saw that." Her gaze rested on him, but it was soft, turned inward. She wasn't really *seeing* him. He could examine her all he wanted now, while she was distracted. "You mean you want me to do the organizing and tell you and Glo what to do, because you know I'll comparison-shop for tinsel." A small, absent smile. Her shoulders relaxed, and for a moment, he glimpsed her happiness again.

She deserved more of it. Much, much more. The only problem was how to discern what would induce such joy.

More gabble-noise. It sounded like the redhead from the coffee shop.

"I can't promise anything, Mayday. I really can't. I'm in the middle of something right now. No, it does *not* have to do with a certain cowboy...no, I am not giving details. Mh." Her gaze clouded. Her left thumb found the bottom of the ring's band, played with its finish. Hal watched, and wished he could feel that slight contact.

She shook her head, an impatient motion, and a single curl brushed her shoulder. "I'll do my best. What? It's not that late—what?" She glanced around, not finding what she sought. "Christ. I should be in bed... *Will* you get your mind out of the gutter? God."

That, apparently, was that. She pressed at the device's face, and sighed, looking down at stacks of paper. "It's past ten," she said, morosely. "I'm done for the day."

"Ah." There was something in his throat. He coughed— that was wrong, he had not done such a thing since he was mortal. "Then you must rest."

"Yeah." She stared at the order she had made out of a mass of chaos. "I wish..."

She caught herself, glancing at him. Shook her head, and went no further.

And Hal, who served desires, found himself almost grateful.

35

RIGHT AND WRONG

IT WAS NO USE.

Em just kept tossing and turning, even though the dove-gray bed was soft and deep, but with *just* the right amount of firmness so her back didn't ache. It was, in a word, perfect, and the sheets didn't cling. They were either just-warm-enough or just-cool-enough, and the pillows were *all* the right shape.

Kind of maddening. You couldn't find anything else to blame for insomnia when your bed was a magical nest of rainbows and kitten fur.

Her eyes were grainy, her mouth tasted awful, and she was so tired. Her muscles all cried out for rest, but her brain wouldn't shut off. It just kept circling back to the man in the black coat—the priest, for God's sake—choking on his own blood. The huge, world-ending noise of the gun. Hal's tortured face running like softened candlewax as she tugged on the hilt of the black-bladed sword.

He rather enjoyed wielding me. Hal didn't even consider himself a person anymore. If he ever had—*I was a slave, there was nothing to want.*

What was it like, to live like that? Could she even imagine?

Yep. Definitely no use. Her conscience had hold of the entire situation and it was speaking loud and clear, just as it always did. It would be so *nice* if she could ignore that quiet, persistent nagging.

Finally, she rolled over and pushed the covers down to her hips. Stared at the gauze swathing the bed. He'd done all this as a *gift*. Someone who would take all that time and care— even if it was magic—deserved more than a fair shake at things.

Hauling herself out of the bed was difficult. She could just lie there, she supposed. Talk herself into donating some of whatever he'd given her to charity and pretend it evened the score. Pretend to be all concerned about him, pretend to be stupider than she was, pretend she didn't know the ring was slipping easily on her finger now. Maybe he had a reason for leading her to think it wouldn't come off—maybe she was a better bet than those Fratres guys.

Magical frat boys. Jesus Christ, the world was bad enough already, it didn't need *that*, too. If they got hold of Hal again, who could tell what they'd do—to him, or to her, or to any sad sack who got in their way?

She could *intend* all the good things she wanted, but sooner or later, she suspected it would get awful easy to mistake *what I want* for *the right thing to do*. That was adulthood in a nutshell.

If she didn't do this now, she might lose her nerve. Not only that, but would she even be able to look at herself in the mirror after a while? Or sit still and smile when May called her "the conscientious one"? How long before she started just arranging things the way she thought they should be? Which was great at the beginning when things were all shiny and new, but it never ended well, in history *or* in fiction.

"God damn it," she muttered. "I'm so goddamn *boring*."

The gauze didn't reply. So she slid her legs out, pushed herself upright, and gave the bed a regretful pat before she padded for the door, bare feet cold against thick carpet.

It took a while to find the kitchen again. Roaming up and down the hallways, peering into other rooms—each in a different color—and finding marvels. A library full of the smell of leather and vanilla-tinged old paper, its door quivering expectantly as she almost, almost stepped in to investigate. A gaming room, with shiny consoles wired to a television screen as big as the wall in her old apartment. An exercise room—she was tempted to whisper *"what, no pool?"* just to see what the house would do.

Not enough bathrooms, and she recognized some of the rooms from magazine layouts. She recognized other things— a couch she'd wistfully circled in a catalog one rainy day while she ate popcorn and half-watched a movie about demons hopping into and out of people, a Seurat print she'd turned the page down at while watching a movie about a time-traveling duke looking to escape a marriage contract. Had he gone through every magazine she had lying around?

It...actually sounded like something he'd do. He seemed a really thorough, belt-and-suspenders type.

So had Steven. But then there was that night, the squeal of tires on wet pavement, and the sickening thud and a crumpled shape on the pavement. Her own breathing, loud in her ears. Him saying, *We could just leave,* and twisting the wheel. Her own horrified gasp, and in that moment their marriage was over. Steven didn't know it then, but that was the split-second she had found out she couldn't live with the man she married. And loved, of course, she would always hurry to add to herself.

She'd even held Steven's hand all through the hearings. The investigation showed the pedestrian was drunker than a skunk after six barrels of cider, and there was no way Steven could have stopped in time. But you never really knew someone until they opened their mouth in a situation like that and said something that showed just how much an alien country lived inside them.

We could just leave.

Her fingers on the seatbelt catch, her door opening on that misty autumn night because he couldn't leave *her* behind, or if he did, he would have to face that choice on his own. She could still remember the smell of crisp leaves sagging under the fog and woodsmoke from someone's chimney.

Why was it always autumn when her life fell apart?

An accident, only an accident. Steven was cleared, and the pedestrian's family didn't want to press charges. They'd even met with him and told him it wasn't his fault. She'd seen Steven through all that, and once it was over, the look on his face when she'd said, *We're getting a divorce.*

He hadn't argued, much. He never had.

The kitchen was brightly lit, and Hal was there, bent over, fiddling with the shiny stainless-steel espresso machine. He turned his head, slightly, and the pleased smile that lit his entire face—now, she recognized the kitchen as the one she'd planned on an Ikea computer a year ago, for God's sake—made her chest feel a little strange.

"Hello, Emily." He just looked so *thrilled*. "Is it morning? You like coffee. I am acquainting myself with this machine in order too—"

"Can we talk?" It came out far more brusque than she intended, and she could have kicked herself, because that shy smile fell right off him so fast it almost shattered on the floor. "Please?"

"Certainly." He straightened, and folded his hands together, lifting them slightly. "I listen, my mistress."

Oh, crap. "Not like that. I mean, really talk." She found

herself fiddling with the ring, nervously. It slipped along awfully easily, really. She twisted it on her finger, and his dark eyes narrowed.

"As you like." He didn't drop his hands, but he did tense up. Those shoulders were really *absurdly* broad. Jeez. A genie could look like whatever he wanted. Had he been watching some of her action-flick DVDs?

She braced herself against the right-hand cabinets. The track lighting was really nice and she could never have afforded it, even if she decided to throw caution to the wind and try some do-it-yourself home renovation. "Okay. Here's the thing." Em took in the deepest breath of her life. "Hal..." It escaped her, just when she'd worked herself up to the sticking-point. "Look. You're...a nice guy." *Way to go with the clichés, Em.*

"If you like." His expression turned shuttered, inward. Closed off. He looked a lot better than when he'd shown up. Wherever he waited between bearers probably didn't have any natural lighting.

She tried again. "Do you...pardon me asking, but do you understand about right and wrong?"

"Right is what my bearer wishes. Wrong is..." He shrugged, a beautiful fluid motion. "Unimportant."

Well, crap. All that power, and no moral compass. This is a bad idea. Really, though, every single choice in this situation was a bad one. So it was, as May always said, time to jump and hope for the best. "But there are things you wouldn't do, if it was up to you. Right?" *Please tell me I'm right.*

"That is...beside the point. I am chained, Emily." A flicker of...something, around his mouth. "Such decisions are not mine to make."

"But hypothetically? Come on, just answer me. Please." *Christ, maybe he's a lawyer, too.*

He spread his hands helplessly; those newly broad shoulders dropped. "Were I left to my own devices, yes, there are things my bearers have asked that I would not have performed."

Relief, hot and acid, went through her. "Great. I just wanted to know. Listen to me. I want to go back to bed and fall asleep. In the morning I want my old apartment back, and my old job back, and *everything* you did there, or to Brett, undone. Okay? I'm not finished."

He'd opened his mouth as if to protest, shut it again so fast she heard his teeth click together and winced afresh. How long was he going to wear that blue sweater? Didn't he ever *sleep?*

Jesus.

She forged on before she could lose her nerve. "And I want you to find that guy—that priest—and make sure he's okay. You said yourself he probably didn't know what you were. Will you do that?"

His chin set. "Yes, mistress."

"Do you *promise?* That no matter what happens between now and when I wake up, you'll do that? All of it?"

"I swear, by my fetter, that I will obey your wishes."

Well, that's going to have to be good enough. "All right." The kitchen floor was too cold. The tiles in here were white with just a ghost of pale peach, bright golden veins running through them. She would have preferred black and white and a small retro cooking area, but he'd done his best. It was kind of endearing, actually. How many other guys, genie or not, would have taken this much time and paid this much attention to small folded-down corners in old catalogs? Em kept twisting the ring, took another step. "Give me your hand. Please."

He froze. "Mistr—Emily. Emily. Don't."

She edged closer. "Please."

He eyed her sideways, a skittish stray cat. "*Don't.*"

Em had the ring worked past her middle knuckle. Even if it shrank now, she could yank it off. What would that do? "Please give me your hand, Hal."

His left hand jumped out, and his entire body had turned rigid. Was he sweating? A sheen lay on his forehead, strange under the bright light.

The ring slid free easily, and she kept a firm hold on his wrist.

The circle of metal was too small for anything but his pinkie. Em's mouth bolted, a runaway train. "You know, with this ring I thee wed, and all that." She slid it onto his smallest finger. "You're free, Hal. And now I'd really like to—" *To fall asleep*, she meant to say.

But there was a rushing noise, and everything went black.

❧ 36 ❧

WAKE UP

NOISE. A THROBBING. NO, A POUNDING. HE HALF-WOKE, then jolted into full awareness as his door—locked, for God's sake, like it was every night—swept open, hitting a carefully left slice of turned-up carpet and slowing. That little bit of insurance was cheap and effective indeed. The old man cursed, and Peter sat straight up, stuffing his left hand under the pillow. He'd let go of the knife, where was the hilt, his damp fingers scrabbled and his skin shrank over his entire body, his balls drawing up as fight-or-flight chemicals poured through him.

His ancestor many times removed jerked the bed's doorward curtain aside with his thin, pasty-white right hand. "Peter! Peter, my boy—"

The glassy hilt closed in his palm, and Peter jerked the blade free. His own hand darted out from under the pillow, and the short, curved, crystalline blade clove air with a low, sweet, deadly sound.

Shit. He hit full consciousness a few seconds after the knife, kissing fabric, tore through the old man's waistcoat, just whispering along the skin underneath.

196

Well, he was committed now. Stupid, stupid, *stupid*. A junior mistake.

The old man threw himself back, dropping into a crouch that was too spry for his wasted frame. "*Peter!*" he spluttered, and Peter tumbled out of the bed, bare feet hitting the Axminster and burning as he lunged.

"*Peter!*" the old man yelled, and perhaps he didn't think his great-great-however-many-greats grandson was quite awake or rational yet.

Oh, I'm awake now. Peter slashed, hearing his mother's screams before she was tranquilized into oblivion. *I've been awake for quite some time.*

If the old man was breaking into his room, either the time had come for him to get rid of Peter or he was too excited to observe any precautions. Either meant that the map had changed, and now Peter could find the ring—

If, that is, he could just *kill* this bastard.

They collided, and now the old man saw the knife. Its blade zinged, a not-quite-audible sound felt more in the teeth than admitted through the ears, and comprehension flashed through the old man's eyes.

Which were, really, very much like his father's. His dead father's.

The old man is dangerous, Peter, his father had said, with the papers for committal on his desk. *It's best this way.*

The old fucker seemed to have octopus arms, for Chris-sake. He writhed in Peter's grasp, one scrawny dead-white hand locked around Peter's right wrist. "Treacherous," he exhaled, foul breath touching Peter's cheek. "*Treacherous* little bastard!"

Mom. Dad. He freed his arm with a galvanic jerk, stabbed wildly. The blade caught flesh, sank in, and the old man howled. The glassblade—it was, said the books, a good way to kill anything immortal, and this one had been a beast to acquire—sang again, and Peter stabbed again. The blade caught on a rib, and the old man sagged, his breathing coming harsh and rancid.

Peter realized he was saying it, over and over, as he plunged the knife home again and again. "Mom. *Dad*. Mom. Dad. Mom Dad Mom Dad MomDadmomdadmomdad *Mommyyyyyyyy*..." He had to stop, whooping in deep, terrible breaths. His arms ached, his pajama pants were twisted around his waist, and something hot and acrid spurted over his hand, slippery and reeking of iron. A hot foulness. Probably the old man's blood had turned to vinegar, or something noxious, just like the rest of him.

When the old man finally sagged and went utterly, sickeningly still, Peter rolled away. He lay on his back, half on cold hardwood, half on carpet that soaked up the sweat all over him. Tears filled his eyes, so he closed them, let the hot salt water trickle down his temples to vanish into his hair.

Mom. Oh, Mom. I did it. I promised I would. I love you, Mom. God.

The only sound was his breathing, just like in a horror movie. He'd often wondered why everyone gasped and panted their way through action flicks, too, but now he knew—it was just what happened. His lungs heaved. Little by little, the frantic throbbing of his heart subsided. His hand ached, ached. He was going to bruise all over, probably.

What a way to wake up. It was the middle of the night; orangish citylight filtered in through the window and turned his room into a collection of half-sensed edges. The map was downstairs. In a minute he would get up, clean himself off, make plans about the body. Then he would—

A slight scratching sound. His eyes flew open. A silver nail descended, slammed through his chest. Something was in his throat, and there was a ringing in his ears.

The old man's face, speckled and starred with a strange,

tarry fluid that was not at all what blood should look like, hovered above him. His ancient claws, both mutilated and whole, were wrapped around the hilt.

"Little bastard," the eldest Cavanaugh hissed into his however-many-times-great-grandson's sweat-wet, dimly surprised face. "You should have taken my head, instead of resting."

The pain was a red-raging beast, but Peter Cavanaugh did not cry out. The sound of a knife buried in meat or chipping bone echoed and re-echoed, a cracked, elderly voice raving about betrayal bouncing off every wall.

But mercifully, for Peter Cavanaugh, everything went dark.

FETTER, CASTLE, BLADE

IT WAS A SMALL, SHABBY PLACE, REALLY. WHY WOULD SHE choose *this* over the palaces he could build? Why not choose to retain some of his gifts? Why would she...

Hal stood over the messy bed, watching. Her breathing came evenly, regular and deep. The flush of healthful sleep was on her cheeks; he had almost, *almost* been unable to hold to substantiality as the roaring filled his ears and the summons to the castle filled every limb with the sharp-sick tingles. Wise of her, to bind him to a promise before she smiled and...

With this ring I thee wed, and all that.

Sometimes, over the long years in the safety of the castle, he had contemplated briefly what it would be like. To be... free. It had never seemed possible, and of course, his knowledge of what *could* free him had been circumscribed. The ones who made him were intelligent enough to plan for that eventuality, and yet in the end, they had been undone by a simple mortal woman.

No, she was not simple. Perceptive, altogether too intelligent for his comfort, and...kind. Kind, to *him*. Dealing with the evidence of the invisible world with far more grace than most, and so determined to do...what?

Do you understand about right and wrong?

There was no need to, when he was fettered. Choice was not a luxury he possessed. Even now, the idea that he could do as he pleased was somewhat...terrifying. His heart thundered in his ears, his palms were slippery with mortal sweat. It was the closest to mortality he had been since they had placed him in the circle and begun their chanting, the heavy incense making him drowsy and the symbols sliced delicately on his skin sending down thin rivulets of blood that caught flying sand, crusting him with stone worn down by infinity.

And go find that priest, make sure he's okay.

He could take that to mean *unable to do further harm*, though he knew she had intended him to be...merciful.

Kindness. And a...morality? It seemed such a bloodless, inelegant word for her dedication to do what she saw as right.

Hal spread his hands. He looked at his palms, their lines shifting a little as his indecision communicated itself into flesh. The ring moved, fingers creaking and the bones sending a sweet lancing pain up his arm as he shifted. When it finished, they had been rearranged, and the ring was now on his third finger, to match how she had worn it. Warm and forgiving, the metal caressed his skin. It was heavy, and he marveled at its weight.

It was a simple matter to fuse it to his own flesh, as he had contemplated fusing it to hers. Why had he not? Had he suspected she would do this, and somehow influenced her?

Lying sprite, Cavanaugh had called him more than once. It was an article of firm belief to the Fratres that a fettered spirit would yearn for vengeance against those who used it. Hal had never given more than he was asked for, and often played the game of fulfilling the letter of a request instead of its intent. *Do not trust the invisible servants,* the grimoires agreed. Perhaps because any slave, substantial or not, would eventually wish for a small measure of liberty.

Emily sighed, moving slightly, and Hal found the knife in his right hand. Plain, wooden-hilted, the blade not metal but flint, sharp as a murderer's whisper. The fetter, the castle, and the blade, all part of his being. Sometimes, in the very inmost core of his being, he had promised revenge on any bearer foolish enough to free him.

Hal leaned forward, slowly. His toes dug in, and as his face lowered, he breathed her in. The scent of clean dark hair, her lucid skin, the hint of her soap, the sandalwood perfume oil she dabbed at her wrists and throat. Simple, subtle, and overwhelming.

"Emily," he whispered, his breath touching her cheek. She did not stir, but she did sigh, a quiet, satisfied sound. The knifehilt, warm and hard, creaked in his fist, squeezed with more-than-mortal strength. The tremors were all through him, tiny shuddering movements as every bearer flashed through his memory, from the very first—the leading sorcerer of the group who had enchained him, his brother who slaughtered him, and on through murders, thefts, new faces spitting commands at him in ancient tongues, all leading to Cavanaugh.

And now, to her. A black-clad woman on a rainy night, with no idea what she had unleashed.

Hal inhaled, deeply, filling his lungs with her. The flint blade slid through silken strands, and when he straightened, he had a single, curling lock of dark hair. There was a priest to catch and some few matters to attend to, before he could enjoy his newfound liberty in the manner he had decided upon.

A few moments later, there was a soft rustling as cardamom-scented air filled the space where he had stood, but no longer was.

✣ 38 ✣

ACADEMIC

HER ALARM SHRILLED. EM REACHED OVER, BASHED THE snooze button with the thoughtless accuracy of long habit, and turned back over to catch fifteen minutes more, burrowed into a warm familiar nest. A dream quivered just at the edge of her waking consciousness, something to do with...

...cardamom breezes and a spur of massive sand-colored rock. Diamond lightning in a story sky as a circle of men chanted all around her, all her skin stinging because she was bleeding, but the pain was faraway and fading just like her own hands turning invisible as she watched.

Her alarm shrilled again, and she fumbled for the switch on the side that would turn it off. Her phone was right there, she checked the calendar.

Thursday. Not a day off. God*damn* it. She was sore all over. Had she been out clubbing with May?

Wait. Hal.

Her stomach almost cramped as she shot upright, her hair standing up in wild curls and her body suddenly a-prickle with goosebumps. She was in a sweatshirt and her Tetris boxers, and even though the elastic on said boxers was popped out and useless, she could have wept with relief.

It was her own shabby, comfortable bedroom, a print of Monet's waterlilies on the wall next to the half-open closet, her clothes hanging in their usual order and her shoes marching along just as they were supposed to. There was her dresser, with the jumble of junk jewelry in a celadon dish and her *real* jewelry box on the other side, a carved cedar beauty that had been her mother's, closed tight and wearing its usual prim smile.

Oh. Em rubbed at her eyes, blinked at her room. Everything was the same. The urge to pinch herself just to make sure she wasn't still dreaming was damn near overwhelming. She slid her feet out of bed, wincing as her body reminded her that she'd either had one hell of a string of hallucinations, or...

Well, let's not think about that. She had to go to work. Everything like it was before, that was the deal. She had to make it to work on time.

Once again, her conscience had fucked her over but good. It would have been nice to wake up in that whipped-cream house and have a couple days of just lounging around.

And getting shot at? You did the right thing, Em.

She didn't bother making her bed, for once, just rubbed her feet against the medium-cheap carpet and shivered at the feeling. Then she hauled herself up, like a cranky old lady, and staggered to the kitchen to flip the coffeepot on.

Her living room was just the same, as if her couch and coffee table and everything else hadn't been shattered. The blank eye of the television regarded her. She should have asked for a better home theater system before he left, really.

It was all a dream. A really vivid one

She'd almost convinced herself as much by the time she shuffled into the kitchen, scratching at her ribs under her ratty, familiar Pigeons sweatshirt. There was a faint familiar smell—Indian food? Maybe. Had she gotten food poisoning and hallucinated? The local health authorities would probably be *very* interested in that, but fuck if she was going to tell them. How would you even begin to report something like that?

Em halted. Her phone was buzzing, back in her room— her you-really-have-got-to-get-up-now alarm. *Belt and suspenders*, her father used to say, usually shaking his head at little Emily's lack of foresight and preparation. He'd really, *really* wanted a Boy Scout of a son, and could never quite get over the fact that his daughter, who tried so hard to make up for her genetic accident, merely suffered camping rather than enjoying it.

Little Emily never quite measured up even now, when she was organized and prepared up the wazoo.

Her eyes were hot, and very full. One scorching, betraying little droplet crawled down her left cheek.

There, on the very clean Formica counter, the sleek silver espresso machine sat.

So he had left her something after all. She couldn't even pretend it was all some sort of Dickensian Christmas fable.

Em scrubbed at her eyes and her cheeks, turned smartly around, and headed for the shower.

THE LINE AT THE COFFEE SHOP ON 158TH WAS ENOUGH TO make her grit her uncaffeinated teeth, her gray raw-silk skirt had a stain on it she didn't remember, her heels rubbed unmercifully, and to top everything off, the spreadsheets were *still* refusing to make sense—someone, somewhere, had done something wrong, and it was up to Em to fix it. Her hair went everywhere, despite the conditioner she'd soaked her head in, and last but *certainly* not least, her phone began buzzing just after the lunch she was forced to skip while tracking down that goddamn data entry error. Not to mention she kept catching herself rubbing at her left ring finger, where there was a small divot.

A small, *empty* divot.

Her phone lit up again. It was May, of course.

Call me, I have the most amazing news!

Looked like Hal had kept his promise. Good for him. Now it was up to May and the Ontario Cowboy, and hopefully they would work it out. Or just bang each other senseless and be buddies afterward. Whichever it was, they could do it without her interference, or even without her commentary for a little while.

Em pinched the bridge of her nose, inhaling. Exhaled a long, tense breath, and when she opened her eyes, the answer to the data-entry bug was right there, staring her in the face.

"Oh," she said, softly. "Well, I'm an idiot."

She'd stumbled on something that could get Brett fired. The trail was there, in the numbers, with his entry codes on payments that shouldn't be. She hadn't been looking in the right place, just assuming the rather *sizable* discrepancy had been from data entry in an entirely different layer.

Well, specializing in Forensic Accounting instead of just taking the basic courses had sounded incredibly interesting. Maybe it was time to go back to school. Meanwhile, she just sat and looked at the screen, absorbing this new turn of events. It was all right to feel a sneaking little sense of joy at karma that was about to land on—

Her sense of victory was short-lived, because a pair of hands descended on her shoulders and *squeezed.*

Emily yelped and dug her heels in, shoving her chair back. It hit the person behind her and there was a clatter, but she had already leapt free and grabbed her stapler. She whirled, and found Brett, blond and slicked-back as ever, had been knocked on his ass. Her chair had fallen on him, and as he struggled to get up, it hit the cubicle-walls on either side of the door opening. They creaked alarmingly, and Becky next door let out a surprised little cry.

Oh, what the flying fucksake... Em ran out of words, even mentally. Brett. Of *course*. She'd almost forgotten about his sneaking little harassing ways. Now, of course, she could wonder if he was sneaking up on her to see if she'd cottoned on to his embezzling. Not only was he a douche, he was a stupid, *creepy* little douche.

She hefted the stapler. He was hopelessly tangled in the chair. First, she could bounce the Swingline off his stupid, pomade-scented head. Then she could stamp on the chair, driving it further into whatever parts of him it could bite. After that, she could pick up her too-old, clunky monitor and drop it on him.

It sounded like a wonderful plan.

"*Ow!*" Brett finally found his breath and yelled.

"Serves you right," Em found herself saying, just as loudly. "Haven't I told you a *million* times not to sneak up on me? Haven't I?" She filled her lungs again, and decided she might as well go for broke. "*Stop trying to touch my breasts!*" she screamed, drowning him out. "*What is wrong with you, are you fourteen? This is not appropriate behavior!*"

Scuttering, scurrying sounds. The entire floor must have heard. Becky's head appeared over the three-quarters wall. "Emily?" Her eyebrows—she'd gotten them waxed, good for her—nested in her hairline, and when she grasped the situation a disbelieving joy spread over her face even as her jaw dropped.

Emily took another deep breath. She caught the sound of hurrying wingtips—it would be Funke. Not even her direct boss, but the one above, the one she'd been worrying about going into a meeting with when she couldn't find the discrepancies.

Oh, my word, it's just like Christmas.

Well, good. *Good.* Her very last nerve had been grated into nonexistence. Once you'd been shot at and set a genie free, an office harasser was *small fucking potatoes.* If she got fired over this—because she knew slimy little bastards like Brett were almost immune from anything, because they had twigs-and-berries—oh well. She had a degree and unemployment. Or maybe she could pack it all in, sell everything, and move to a hot country where the cost of living was ridiculously low.

Once you stopped caring about being polite, things got so much easier. And if she was going to get the stupid, inconvenient as *fuck* parts of behaving ethically, she might as well have some fun with the rest of it.

"*I do not want to date you!*" She pitched this just under a yell, but in the hush, it was a klaxon. Brett had gone dead-white, and his mouth moved a little. She lifted the stapler, and his gaze focused on it.

The look of sudden fear on his bland, blond, plastic face was incredibly satisfying.

"What's going on here?" Funke scurried around the corner, his potbelly preceding him. Today he wore a blue pinstripe suit, but his tie was askew and his scalp glowed through the few graying strands he combed religiously over its dome. In meetings he was always rather gentle, but his interdepartmental maneuverings were said to rival a shark's.

"Him." Em pointed the stapler at the supine, now-quivering Brett. "That's what's going on here."

"What the..." Funke started smoothing his tie. He did it whenever a meeting veered off track, too, and Em's irritation reached truly cosmic levels she hadn't felt since high school. "What on *earth* is he doing on the floor?"

"Trying to steal my office chair." It was as good an explanation as any. She grabbed for her purse *and* her coat, scooping her phone up. There wasn't much room, but as soon as she twitched in Brett's direction, he began frantically squirming away. One of the chair's arms speared him in the groin, and his writhing was, she could not lie, deeply satisfying.

"Where are you going?" Funke swayed from foot to foot, trying to process this. "Emily? It's Emily, right? Where are you—"

"Becky." She half-turned. "Check the payments on the 88-C1 sheets. Brett here has been embezzling from the company."

Becks shut her mouth with a snap. At least no moss grew on *her*. Dawning comprehension lit her face. "That's why they weren't lining up!"

"You're welcome." Em stepped over one of Brett's legs. "Mr. Funke, Becky can show you exactly what's been going on. I suggest you fire this guy, but that's academic." Another deep breath of stale air, the boiled coffee in the break room, cheap hard-as-nails nylon carpet adding its own scratchy component to the mix.

It smelled a lot like freedom.

"Academic—" Funke was struggling to catch up.

"I can explain!" Brett all but howled, but Becky was already back in her chair, pulling up the requisite sheets. Maybe she'd get a nice raise from this. Maybe, just maybe, Brett would be fired and the good guys would have won a round. Maybe things would work out the way they were supposed to.

It could all happen without her, though. She was *done*.

"Yes, academic." Em settled her purse on her shoulder as her phone quit buzzing. *Oh, May, do I have a story to tell you.* "Because *I quit*."

🕮 39 🕮

SHOWS MERCY

It took longer than he liked—almost a day of patient tracking—to find the dying priest. Finally, though, his patience—and a healthy dose of luck—led him to the seething mass of a poorer part of the city and a motel that rented, from the look of it, by the hour. So soon he had begun to distinguish what they called poverty; its glaring amid the rest of the plenty was obscene in a way no other mortal act could approach. The tall, dispirited building all but slumped on its bones, its parking lot jammed with the cheaper types of cars and a reek of tobacco smoke, exhaust, and desperation as well as burned food in each corner.

It was, Hal thought, a terrible place to die.

Tied to a severe wooden chair that had to be brought into existence to serve Hal's need, the lean, black-clad priest blinked groggily. Possessed of a broken nose, bruising around both eyes, and with his mouth slack from the drugging incense Hal had wrapped this entire small room in, he looked even younger than he had before. Only mortal, after all. And his faith did not proof him against sorcery older than his pale, meek, risen corpse-god.

Take care of him. Make sure he's okay.

It was almost miraculous the man had managed to retreat here, considering the amount of internal damage Hal had inflicted. Perhaps he could thank his god for it.

Hal's hands plunged into the priest's body. Rearranging, melding, cauterizing, sealing the worst damage, reshaping the organs into their proper configurations and settling them back in their cavities. He could have done this invisibly, true.

But he wanted the man to *feel* it.

"*Diabolus...*" The priest coughed, blood spraying from his lips. "They...said *witch.* Jezebel's Brood."

"Your kind are still murdering women for that old tale?" Hal shook his head. His fingers tensed, and the priest screamed, a low hoarse sound robbed of its true volume by the fact that one of his lungs was half-full of fluid. "And you would have killed *her.*"

"They...*proof*..." He stiffened, and Hal exhaled, a long slow sound that filled the room with cardamom and smoke.

Power leapt to obey him, cleansed the stink of blood and loosed bowels, and he drew his hands slowly from the mortal man's body. "Their proof does not concern me." He let the man breathe a little, glancing up at the window. The curtains —cheap, mass-produced, but still more solid than many in rich homes of Cavanaugh's time—ruffled a little as they felt his attention. It was a good thing Emily was not here. She would glow against this backdrop like the pearl she was, but a gentle woman should not see what he had done.

Perhaps she would even be disappointed. He had set out to heal the man, certainly.

But he had not done it painlessly.

The mortal sagged in the chair, the ropes holding him upright. His eyes glittered, feverish but sharper now that the agony was receding. The tattooed picture on his chest—the face of a condemned man hung on an instrument of torture—

peered out through his torn-open cassock and the white shirt beneath; they were covered with dried blood, vomit, and other matter. *"Deus,"* he whispered. *"Deus, misericors—"*

"I am not your god. Nor am I one of your demons." Hal stood, unfolding slowly. "The woman you would have killed asked me to spare your life. That shows mercy, does it not?"

To give him credit, the mortal did not beg. He did not even look hopeful. His chin rose defiantly. He coughed, the fluid burbling in his lungs. This place had a filthy sink, an even filthier commode, and the bed was ridden with vermin.

Yes, Emily should never see something like this. Even this world, so clean and full of marvels, was not, at its heart, very different from Cavanaugh's. One had merely to dig, to lift a corner of a curtain, and gaze underneath to find the squirming of maggots.

Hal *focused.* The priest retched and a slick flood of clear fluid tinged with crimson poured from his mouth and nose. When it was over he heaved and gasped, sucking sweet, blessed air in.

He waited for the priest's breathing to even out a bit. "I shall ask you only once, priest, and should you choose not to answer, her mercy will not apply." Hal gazed down into the mortal's face. "The names of those who hired you. Their locations. All the information you possess that will lead me to them."

He did not add that he could tear the knowledge from the mortal by force. It was only a question of method, and how... merciful...Hal wished to be.

Do you know the difference between right and wrong?

"They..." The priest coughed, rackingly. His ribs, no longer shattered, moved as they should, and he squirmed uncomfortably in the chair. "Sophics *lied.*"

"Yes." Hal clasped his hands, rubbing his second right finger over the ring's stone. It was a pleasant sensation, to remind himself he was free. He waited on no command but his own.

"Do you swear...in the name of our Father, and by Solomon, *Yevjoha-eh, Elohim?*" Another string of syllables garbled into incomprehensibility by ancient, finger-sore monks tracing them laboriously in tomes kept under lock and key, the secrets of a Church intent on retaining temporal power by any means necessary.

Even the worst.

The words almost made him laugh. Gibberish, even though someone involved must have some talent because the man's bullets had borne a charge of power. Hal nodded, taking care to keep his expression serious. "I swear on your God, the god of the brothers of your Order of Saint Bartholomew and the Redemption, that those who hired you sent you to kill an innocent."

In all senses of the word.

"Murderers." The priest's face lit with dull anger. It was amazing he had enough blood left to suffuse his cheeks with such color. "Apostates."

Hal listened as the words continued. He was physical, now, and the words spilling from the man's mouth turned him cold. The Fratres had indeed sent this man, and lied quite convincingly to him. For them to take such a risk...

He had left subtle, invisible safeguards upon a sleeping Emily, but they would not be enough. As the man continued babbling, spilling names, Hal inferred even more from what was left unsaid, and what the priest conjectured. Her last...request...of him would muddy the tracks leading to her door, but the Fratres had expended this much effort, there were certainly more nasty surprises meant for his former—no.

His bearer. His *Emily*.

"And I swear on Christ's holy wounds," the priest finished, his teeth grimed with blood and a crust at each corner of his mouth, "that I shall visit vengeance upon them for their lies, their corruption, their—"

Oh, that is very good. Hal interrupted. "Yes." He made a slight inward motion, and the bonds holding the man in the chair slip-slithered, snakelike, free, coiling watchful on the floor. "I rather think you will. Tell me one last thing, priest."

"Get thee behind me," the man whispered. His eyes had grown round. They begged for miracles until they *saw* them, his kind. Then they reached for their weapons.

And that suited Hal's purposes nicely. "What do you need, in order to accomplish your vengeance? Speak quickly."

❧ 40 ❧

COMPLICATED

"YOU DID *WHAT?*" MAY'S JAW DROPPED. EM MOTIONED HER in so she could shut the door. The takeout containers on the counter sent up a lovely steaming smell of Chinese food. Moo goo gai pan, General Tso's chicken, broccoli beef. She'd even gotten eggrolls, because god damn it, if her ship was going down she was going to enjoy herself before the waves came over the deck.

Em winced. Her imagination just worked a little too well. "I quit." Getting into yoga pants and another sweatshirt had been the only redeeming feature of the whole damn day.

"Uh." May, unwinding a chartreuse scarf from her ruddy head, went straight for the cabinet over the fridge, lifting herself on very tip-toe and feeling about for the emergency booze.

Em locked the door and tried not to sigh too loudly. "It's on the counter. Eat first, please."

May let out a long, low whistle. "Wow, swanky! When did you get the espresso beast here?"

"Bonus from work." Em headed for the bottle of Laphroaig on the counter. Another jolt of it would go down really well right about now. She'd already had one waiting for May to arrive, and the comforting warmth in her empty stomach was very nice but wouldn't last long.

"Right before you quit?" May's coppery eyebrows went up. Today she was even a little conservative—black swinging skirt, black tights, a hot-pink velour top and her hair piled atop her head with careless artistry. Except for her bacon-and-egg earrings. Those were pure May, and a relief to see.

Em shrugged. "It's...complicated."

"I'll bet." May whirled on her toes, set her heels down firmly, and scrutinized Em from top to toe. "Start at the beginning."

I can't. "Why don't you go first? You said you had news." Em realized she was punking out as soon as she said it.

May eyed her, the sunny smile falling away and that serious, pinched look—the same one worn when Em finally admitted outright she was divorcing Stephen—turning her at least ten years older. "No," she said finally. "You don't get to do that."

Huh? "Do what?"

"Redirect me like that. You quit your *job*. That's like the Pope turning Scientologist."

"Wouldn't that be a trick. Come on, this'll get cold." But Em halted, crossing her arms defensively.

"You've been weird since the party." May's forehead was well and truly wrinkled now, and she had that look. That terrier-sees-a-rat look, the expression that meant flighty, irresponsible May was about to indulge in one of her fits of stubborn poking because she knew something was off, goddammit, and she was going to find out what. "Did something happen?"

"I got a little drunk, that's all." The conversation was *not* going the way Em had intended. "Look, May, I've had a really...a really bad day, I need to come down from it before I go over the chowder-to-cashews, and I want to hear some good news. Which I'm suspecting you have."

"So it *was* you." May grinned, but the shadow of worry didn't leave her big baby blues. "You sneaky little bitch."

"He's been calling me asking for your number, I just haven't been able to pick up. What's his name, Jake? What's he like with clothes on and coffee in his manly paw?" Em reached for the cupboard that held the plates. "Tell me how it went and if you like him, then I'll spill my guts."

"Promise?"

"I promise," Em lied. She'd already decided no word of a genie was going to cross her lips. The last thing she needed was May actively doubting her sanity.

She was doing that just fine on her own. Even, and *especially,* with the damn espresso machine sitting there, gleaming and secretive.

"I'm going to hold you to that." May got down tumblers, slopping amber liquid into both of them, and Em winced again. The last thing she wanted was another hangover. Although...if getting drunk had started this, maybe a bender would make it all go away? "So," her best friend continued, rustling the bag and peering at the takeout cartons, "I see *your* standard order hasn't changed. And there's eggrolls, you must be feeling daring. What did you get me?"

"Moo goo gai pan."

"I love you. Marry me." May batted her eyelashes, took a hit off the Scotch, and began her tale of walking into her usual coffee spot a bit early because this Thursday had turned out to be a half day...and finding Jake the Ontario Stripper in pressed khakis and a buttondown, tongue-tied and blushing. It was a good thing she'd only been scheduled to work in the morning, because she didn't go back to the office. They'd ended up at the aquarium, naming all the fish things like

Bertie and Megalookoko, and May had another date with him tomorrow night.

Sushi, of course.

Em listened, made interested noises, and asked all the right questions. All the time, picking at her General Tso's, she was trying to come up with an explanation that didn't sound like she'd lost her goddamn mind.

"So now it's your turn." May set down her chopsticks and took another sip of Scotch. "Start at the beginning."

"I...I bought this—"

Oh, crap, Emily realized. I'm about to tell her the truth.

She braced herself, but just as she did there was a soft, polite trio of raps, and Emily's heart leapt up into her throat. *It's him. He's come back.*

But that was stupid. He would just *appear*, wouldn't he? And why should *that* particular prospect make her feel funny and lightheaded and sort of...

"Wait a second," she said, and May was already on her feet, turning to look at the balcony door. Dark had fallen, and their reflections were moving, because the slab of glass was sliding smoothly along its runners.

"Is someone hiding on your—" May sounded delighted at the prospect, and Em lunged for the breakfast counter. Her phone, and May's, were right there.

Pop! A sharpness, burying itself in her back.

What the fuck? She grabbed for her phone, her fingers turning into clumsy sausages. Her back was suddenly very warm, something spreading from whatever had hit her. Was she shot? She didn't hear anything—

May let out a horrified gasp. There was another *thock*, and Em's feet tangled together. She went down hard, her head just missing the edge of the counter. Everything turned blurry.

"Yes," a man said. One crisp little word. Something

nudged her shoulder, and her body wouldn't obey her. She spilled onto her back, staring through the sudden fuzz.

Lank, very dark hair, way too long, falling in ratty strings around a thin, dead-white face. He was skinny and very pale, and there were pockmark scars on his cheeks. The gun he was holding—a rifle, maybe, pointed at the ceiling like they did in action movies—looked very big, and the way he handled it showed little familiarity and a lot of distaste. His mouth moved, but it took a while for the words to come through the warm, soft cottonwool filling her head.

"Well, that is rather a bit too much." He was wearing, of all things, a dark suit that looked like a tuxedo, and clicked his tongue a little. His left hand, hanging at his side, twitched.

The first finger on that hand was a small, long-healed stump.

41

PRETEND TO BE MORTAL

THE FIRE ROARED, TAKING A DEEP BREATH OF COOL NIGHT air. Hal grabbed the priest's arm and hauled them both *sideways*, dancing through time and space at once. They resolved into the physical *just* outside a building the sign proclaimed as Charenton Hall, which was also burning merrily. Inside were financial records and all manner of paperwork, which Hal had absorbed quite handily after a group of security officers had been dealt with.

The grenades the priest had supplied were gloriously efficient. Hal could even see the utility of manufacturing them in certain situations, now that he grasped their chemical components.

The tall man in smoke-tarnished black bent over, retching. Hal patted him on the back, once, twice. "Are you hurt?"

A quick shake of the priest's sandy head. He was wet with sweat, flushed with fire-heat, and had expended quite a bit of effort. This was one of their more important buildings, and the guards had been armed. Some of the dangers inside the blazing shell had not been quite physical, too.

Hal had learned much from watching the priest work.

"You really are quite admirable." He waited for the man to catch his breath. Sirens began in the distance, and an explosion deeper in the building sent a column of nasty black smoke up to the iron-gray, ice-weeping sky.

What was Emily doing at this moment? Perhaps she was in her apartment, comfortable out of the damp, in those pants with strange animals patterned on them and that very large, thick sweatshirt.

Hal put the thought away. She would not be truly safe until he finished this night's work. The Sophic Fratres, both their inner and outer circles, were neutralized. Or at least, they would be once he and the priest attended to one more address. The organization had grown large, its tentacles sinking in all over the world, but they had also used computers to organize much of that growth.

Once Hal had peered into that fascinating chain of electrons and found the patterns, he had little time to do anything other than search for the most damaging information while the priest held the guards at bay. The physical buildings were only shells now, the hidden and quite illegal parts of the Sophics' network now laid bare to the relevant mortal authorities. While their arcane and esoteric crimes were beyond the mortal law's purview, several of their financial interests were *not*.

Nor were some of the leaders' peccadilloes, mostly sexual but in one or two places truly repugnant. How little things changed.

The priest heaved again, a dry, hideous sound. "God... *damn* you, don't...*do* that."

"Would you rather have been burned alive?" Yes, he rather liked this man, Hal decided. He might even have been a good bearer. "One left," he said. "Are you ready?"

"No." The priest straightened. "Ammo. I need ammo—"

"Ah." A moment's concentration, and Hal nodded. "There."

"Are you *sure* you're not a demon?" The priest—his name was Frank, Hal reminded himself—crossed himself. He had not, however, loosened his grip on his suddenly-heavier pistol. A well-designed machine.

Both of them.

"Very." The thought of Em, sleeping trustfully in her rumpled, shabby bed, would not retreat. What would she do when he reappeared? Perhaps he should wear another face, pretend to be mortal? Would that make it more comfortable for her? "I was once a mortal man too, Priest."

That bit of information seemed to unseat the man's stomach again. "What happened?"

"*They* did." Hal indicated the burning building, with a short jab of his chin. It was as good an explanation as any. There were always those who sought to use whatever—and whoever—was to hand. "Long, long ago, before your Church."

That earned him a mistrustful sidelong glance, but the man was breathing much more easily now. In the end, the priest contented himself with a simple, neutral observation. "The police will be here soon."

Which was probably wise.

"Yes. Are you ready?"

Frank shook his head, but Hal had closed his fingers around the man's wrist. The power rose in a shimmering curtain, and the ice-dappled sidewalk was empty well before the first fire engine's headlights appeared.

IT WAS LIKE STEPPING THROUGH TIME AGAIN, BUT FURTHER than *he* could even with the powers granted him. The rotunda, the sweeping staircase, the suits of armor on their stands—all familiar, and the incense smell was familiar as well. Clearly, someone was a traditionalist. The most secret of the Sophic houses in Cavanaugh's time had looked very much like this.

Muffled chanting behind heavy double doors. They were at work, it seemed.

Beside him, Frank the priest bent over, trying to contain his retches. This method of travel was difficult for those not accustomed. Emily had displayed a similar reaction, but much more graceful.

Hal closed his corporeal eyes, *feeling* about the building. Yes. The priest had been right. This was their center of power in the city. The transition to a new continent had meant much opportunity, and they had seized it. Clever mortals, indeed.

He patted the man's back again, alleviating what he could of the nausea and making doubly certain he hadn't left any of the man's internal organs behind. It paid to be thorough.

"*Christos*," Frank whispered. He was paper-pale, and it took him a few minutes to regain himself. "Will you *stop* doing that?"

"If you would prefer to walk, I can accommodate you." Hal's mouth tilted up at one end. Strange, to wear such an expression. Emily might have been pleased to see it. "Listen."

The priest closed his eyes now, struggling to contain his runaway breath. He stilled, and for a moment, that was almost concerning. Almost as motionless as Hal himself could be. "Sorcery," he breathed. "Is *this* not diabolical?"

"I believe this ritual dates from 1548." Hal kept his own voice low. "Which could possibly make it so, according to your Order's standards. No, do *not* try to disturb it." He hauled the man back. "You will be occupied with the *other* guards."

"Which are?" Frank the priest's sandy eyebrows rose, and Hal let himself look up the stairs, where the smokesteam shimmers of very nasty apparitions were beginning, scenting mortal meat and blood. "Oh," Frank continued, wry realization filling his tone. "They're right behind me, aren't they."

Very intelligent. "Once I let go of you, they will attack. You should be able to fend them off." Hal exhaled softly. "Are you ready?"

"God protect us," Frank whispered. "Yes."

"Good man." Once he finished with the circle of Fratres behind the great door, he could return to Emily.

He could, perhaps, wait as she slept, and make coffee when she woke. It sounded like...well, no doubt, Frank the priest would call it heaven.

Hal let go.

❦ 42 ❦

BE PRECISE, POPPET

IT WORE OFF IN STAGES. EM SURFACED SLOWLY, HER HEAD aching and her shoulder on fire. She tried to move, but something bit her wrists, and she blinked several times, trying to make sense of what she was seeing. What was happening.

Why do I suspect nothing will make sense ever again?

"You're awake," he said, harshly. "Good." A crisp accent, the words almost sounding foreign. He gripped her shoulder, rolling her onto her back; Em winced, a small sound driven out of her because her hands were tied behind her and it was *not* comfortable. Someone else was gasping, and there was a sharp sour stink of vomit.

"Your friend is quite the wild one." His face thrust close to hers, and she smelled a screen of minty toothpaste over the furred stench of onion rot, an expensive aftershave, and a strange coppery stink. "In my day, she'd be taught some respect. Come on, up with you." He had hazel eyes, a nose that would have been proud if not for the bulb on the end of it, and for some reason, she knew she *must* know who he was, even though she'd never seen him before. Those scars on his cheeks...

Smallpox, she realized. *He wouldn't have had a vaccination, now would he.*

He hauled her upright. Her legs didn't want to work, but he was stronger than he looked. He shoved her down into the couch, and the gasping was from May on the floor in front of the television, her eyes closed. The vomit-smell was from her —a puddle of it spread from her best friend's mouth, and there was a bruise spreading up the left side of her face. A deep, dark-red one.

He hit May. Em cleared her throat. "George...Cavanaugh... I presume?" Her tongue didn't quite fit in her mouth; the rest of her face was numb. She sounded drunk. *That was a tranquilizer gun. Jesus Christ.*

He looked pleased for a bare moment before his mouth drew itself into a tight, prissy little line. "Well. A bright little doll you are. Where is your husband?"

What? "I'm divorced." Good God, just imagining Steven trying to deal with this was enough to make her want to laugh, albeit in a weird, screechy, hysterical sort of way. Steven's conflict resolution was nonviolent to the max. "It's not here."

"What?" Cavanaugh glared at her, and the mad gleam in his hazel eyes told her he was two tons past crazy and not slowing down anytime soon.

She took a deep breath, propping herself against the couch arm. A real charmer, no wonder Hal hadn't liked this guy. "You're going to...try to torture me into...telling you where the ring is."

He drew himself up. He was short and more than a little bandy-legged—malnutrition or some childhood disease, maybe? The tuxedo looked like it had been mothballed in the twenties. And instead of the tranquilizer gun, now he had a knife.

It was thin, and pointed, and looked like it was made of

glass. Or some kind of clear rock, but there wasn't any knapping on the blade. His right hand, pale and spidery, clutched the leather-wrapped hilt. His left, with its mangled first finger, shot out and clamped on her shoulder. "Do I have to torture you, poppet?"

No, you don't. But you look like you'd like to. "It's *not here*." She was beginning to get her breath back. And, wouldn't you know, her bladder suddenly felt two sizes too small. Either she had a UTI or something about being in dire danger made her want to wee-wee like mad.

"No husband. Then a paramour?" He cast a glance over her apartment. "Who keeps you here? You could do better, you know."

"What?" The urge to tell him to *speak English, for God's sake* rose and was ruthlessly strangled in the same instant. She was looking at a man who had been alive before electricity was discovered. Almost before the steam engine, maybe.

It didn't look like he'd put the intervening time to good use.

"The man. Who has my ring." He touched her cheek with the knifetip. It was very sharp, and very cold. "Your lover, or whatever he is to you. Where is he?"

What the... It dawned on her that he maybe didn't even realize *she'd* been the one to wake Hal up. He just figured there had to be a man somewhere, and she was an afterthought. Or he assumed she'd given the ring to a man, because...why?

Who the fuck knew?

Think fast, Em.

"Do you think he'll still fancy you with an eye put out?" He grinned, baring discolored, crooked teeth that were nevertheless strong. One of his molars on the bottom left was missing. It was a wonder he wasn't missing more, judging by his halitosis. Maybe he'd brushed before coming out to climb into her apartment? Could she imagine him going in to get braces?

Did this guy floss? Her brain kept shying away from the situation, serving up the strangest and most *unhelpful* goddamn things.

The knifetip drifted up. Slowly. Em swallowed, hard. "Look." She tried to lean away from the knife, an instinctive movement, but his left hand crawled up into her hair and grabbed a handful, tensing. The nubbin of his mutilated finger dug into her scalp; her stomach gave a loose, weird shake inside her, as if she was going to projectile puke all over him. *Don't you dare, Em.* "That's my friend. She has no part of this. Let her go, and I'll tell you where it is."

May groaned, a long liquid sound ending with a slurred "—sonofa*bitch.*" Her eyelids fluttered.

"Oh, so now you know where my property lies? Out with it." The tip jabbed, high up on her cheek, and the pinprick welled with heat.

Oh, God. She couldn't even look at May. His face filled up her field of vision, sweat along his temples, lank brown hair matted at the ends. Blackheads festered on either side of his nose, but the worst was his *eyes.* Hazel, bloodshot, and completely normal on the surface. It wasn't until you got this close that you saw the complete, utter madness shining in the depths of his pupils.

"I can show you," she hedged. Her eyes felt naked, and the knifepoint lingered, a tiny hot welling tiptoeing down her cheek. She stared at him, her pulse thundering in her ears. A rushing noise began, trying to seep in and fill her head.

Stop that. May. Think of May. Keep her safe.

"And I can carve your face like a turnip, poppet. *Where is my ring?*" He shouted the last bit, his breath swarming over her face, and Em flinched. The knife dug a little more, and the trickle down her cheek fattened.

"You *bastard*," May said, slurred but still recognizable. "Fuck off!"

Oh dear. "May!" *For Chrissake, can't you be quiet for once in your life and let me—*

Cavanaugh shifted. He pulled the knife back, jabbed it over his shoulder in May's general direction. His hand twisted in Em's hair, pulling viciously, tearing some strands free. "Or I can carve your foul-mouth little dagget of a friend. Which do you prefer?"

"It's *not here*!" The words burst out of her. "I gave it to Hal!"

Silence, except for May's harsh breathing and her own.

Cavanaugh let go of her hair. He straightened, and the knife retreated. "To whom? Be precise, poppet."

Oh, what the fuck. Maybe if he knew it was completely gone, he'd...what? Climb out the window and leave them alone? Maybe he'd just kill *her* and May could get away? "May? May, are you all right?"

"What a party," her best friend slurred. She coughed, wetly. "Jesus *fuck.*"

Yeah. Like she'd be able to fight this maniac off or run. Maybe if Em screamed—

The slap came out of nowhere, smashing her head to the side, her non-bloody cheek on fire now. Then Cavanaugh's fingers were in her hair again. He wrenched her head back, and the knifepoint rested against her throat.

So sharp. So sharp it was *cold.* Probably would go right through her like butter.

Hot knife through butter, isn't that the saying?

He was very quiet now, and the only thing worse than the pseudo-politeness in his tone was the sense that he was already considering whether or not to stab them both. "To whom did you give my ring? Answer me, and I might decide to leave you and your whore friend still breathing." His breath brushed her cheek. A bubble of something hot and bilious lodged in her throat. She had to cough, didn't want to. Swallowed, wished she hasn't because the point of the knife was *right there*.

"I gave it to Hal," she whispered. "The genie. The *spirit*. I put it on his finger. He's free."

The knife fell away. So did his hand in her hair, and Em almost sobbed with relief.

"You...what?" Cavanaugh's throat worked vigorously for a few seconds. "You did *what?*"

Maybe I can kick him. Her head was swimming from the tranquilizer, a flat copper mallet pounding in the back of her throat. *And somehow get the knife.*

Sure. With her hands tied behind her back and her ankles tied, too. Right.

"You did *what?*" he repeated, and slapped her again. This time it was her bloody cheek, and it was more like a punch because he'd closed his fist around the knifehilt to brace it. The force of the blow tipped her over on the couch, and the world went white for a few seconds.

When she came to, she heard someone yelling.

It was her own voice. "—you do to him, you sonofabitch! He didn't *ask* to be stuck in that ring, he didn't *ask* to be a slave!"

"SHUT UP!" Cavanaugh roared, his knees on either side of her supine body, lifting the blade overhead.

The glass blade glittered as it plunged down, sinking to the hilt with an odd, meaty sound. For a second Em could only think *that's odd, it doesn't hurt* before the pain began, and it did.

It hurt plenty.

May kept screaming.

❧ 43 ❧

BEST YOU LEAVE NOW

THE PRIEST HAD SUNK TO ONE KNEE, HIS FOREHEAD against his hand on the hilt of his strange black-bladed sword. Hal flicked his fingers, dismissively, and blood spattered, smoking in the sudden chill. Every battlefield smelled the same; the only differences were the exact degree of smoke and the language the wounded cried out weakly in.

And the silence, when they were done.

Hal straightened, taking a deep breath. The smoke was beginning to thicken. There were no cries.

He had left no wounded.

"Are you injured?"

"Gonna feel this tomorrow." Frank's breathing came in deep heaves. His sandy hair tangled over his forehead, strands glinting gold in the electric light. His cassock was rent and torn; it had stood up admirably under the night's assaults, much like its owner.

"Not necessarily. Would you like to forget this entire incident? It is possible, you know." Hal glanced at the ruins of the sanctum doors. Behind them, the bodies of the men gathering sorcerous force lay in twisted, shattered ruins. It was, to put it mildly, a mess.

"Oh, no. Don't tempt me with that." Frank heaved himself up, groaning a little. Tested his right ankle—his boots were quite well designed, and Hal had taken note of their structure to clothe himself in a similar pair. When the priest was certain he could stand, he drew himself up, put more weight on his ankle, and winced afresh. "My superiors will want to know about this. The Sophics, meddling in the forbidden and trying to use *us* to clean up." He grimaced again. There was a stippling of gunpowder on his cheek, and it was quite likely the blood in his hair was at least partly his own. "Perhaps they'll set me to hunting down the rest of them."

"Perhaps they will." Hal's smile felt...genuine. "And me?"

"Far as I can see, you're no *diabolus*." The priest eyed him speculatively. "Perhaps I'll carry a sin of omission."

"Balanced against all the souls you have saved?" Hal watched the man's hand. Any change in his grip would require a...response. Something was burning, flames perfumed with bricks of ceremonial incense dancing inside the Sanctum. Someone had indeed known the old recipes; Hal had not smelled that particular blend since Cavanaugh's last meeting with his Fratres. The heavy draperies would catch in a little while. "I have other business tonight."

"The woman. The innocent." The priest's mien grew severe, and his grasp on the hilt firmed. "Tell me you mean her no harm."

"Harm?" Hal shook his head. "*This* is all for her safety." He paused. *And she will never know.* "Friend, I think it's best you leave now."

Frank nodded. Smoke curled from the shattered double doors behind Hal. The rest of the building was now full of torn cloth and fragments of furniture. Soon, it would be ashes. "I think so too." He did not say *God watch over you*, or even that absurdity, *God bless you*.

Instead, he simply turned, and began picking his way for the front door. He weaved perhaps a little bit more than was acceptable, swaying with exhaustion.

Hal reined his irritation. He spread his hands, and the power filled him.

The least he could do was make sure the man was safe. And heal the worst of his wounds.

Emily, after all, might have wanted as much.

HE COULD HAVE APPEARED IN THE MIDDLE OF HER FLAT, but that might have startled her. Hal glanced down at himself again. Jeans. Sweater. No blood on cloth or skin, no stain of the violence he had sunk into, except those marvelous boots, clean now and very decorous indeed. The ring gleamed on his finger, and he stood outside the door to her small, shabby home. He could have slid right through, as he had that first morning, but...

He checked himself again. Yes, he was clean. Unbloody. What did a hero of those marvelous novels do?

Ah. He lifted a hand to knock. Halted, his head tilted slightly and his face changing by degrees.

Sounds filtered through the thin pasteboard door. Whimpering. A thudding noise.

Then, inside Emily's home, a woman began to scream.

The door shivered into splinters as he propelled himself through it, forgetting that he could thin out into insubstantiality. The short hall was nightmare-long, twisting, and the sound kept going, on and on.

Cavanaugh. His first sight of the man in so long, and he looked just the same. Except instead of wide breeches, hose, and square lace collar, it was a spare dark suit of a more modern cut. The man lifted a dripping knife, its blade a hurtful glassy gleam. The scrawny, ancient mortal looked up as Hal burst through, and there was Emily's red-haired friend, hands and feet bound, on the floor in front of the television. There was the stink of some acrid medication in the air—had Cavanaugh poisoned both of them? It was likely. How?

Did it matter?

The back of the couch barred Hal's view of whatever Cavanaugh was savaging, bright beads of blood hung in the air, and Hal's silent, internal scream twisted most of the room sideways from the timestream. Just a fraction.

Just enough.

The room quivered, restive, as he stepped forward. Was the floor moving? No, he was reeling as if he was mortal-drunk.

While he had been at work, his former bearer had too.

Cavanaugh's pockmarked, pale face was splashed with blood, and his hair was lank and foul. His mangled left hand had risen, flung to the side as he lifted the blade in his right. It was a *sacr'pell*, a glassy Knife of Ending, and it could perhaps do Hal a mischief were it buried in his own guts. It could certainly kill Cavanaugh—it was one of the few things that would bite his throat, did its wielder have the sense to decapitate the beast.

Stillness. Quiet. The timestream plucked at the edges of his control. He reached the back of her slumping, shabby, very comfortable brown couch, and looked down.

Emily.

His bearer lay half on her back, pale and still. Her sweet, lucent cheek was dewed with bright crimson. Her hair was a glory of tangled curls, but the bindings at her ankles cut cruelly. They were plastic, wicked little things meant to cinch tight and become impossible to loosen. Her wrists were probably similarly bound, trapped helpless underneath her.

So much blood, and...chips of glaring white bone. Her eyes were half-closed, and the spark of life trembled in its violated container.

Quickly now. Delicate work, to keep her in stasis so that spark did not flee to more congenial climes.

The room shook and spun at that thought, and Hal clamped down, fiercely. *No.*

The glassy knife trembled, giving off a high thin singing sound of strain. It wanted more. It had been used for murder in the recent past, longed to be used so again. It fought Hal's grip on the stream. His hands gripped the back of the couch, wood and stuffing and fabric melting under his will.

The spark, a bright serene point of light caught in Emily's broken, beautiful mortality, guttered.

No. Do not leave me.

Her voice, soft and sweet. *I thee wed, and all that...do you know the difference between right and wrong?*

He was too old, and had been chained far too long, to know. If there was a distinction, she would have to teach it to him.

And for that, she had to be alive.

Hal *moved.*

☙ 44 ❧
WORTHY OF WHAT WAS
GIVEN

THE WORLD TURNED OVER. EM HIT THE FLOOR, HARD, ARMS and legs suddenly free. She choked, coughing, and rolled, a giant warm hand shoving her along. The coffee table was smashed aside with a muffled *crack*, splinters flying, but none of it touched her. Whatever was pushing her along had simply batted it out of the way. She came to a breathless, tumbled halt right next to May, whose mouth was ajar and a tiny whispering scream struggling for release, her blue eyes wide and terrified. The puddle of vomit had disappeared, and the living room was full of a vast rustling quiet.

And the fiery, furious scent of burning cardamom.

"You," Hal said quietly.

He stood in the middle of the ruin of Em's couch, and she felt only a weary wonder that she was alive. Something had happened in the past few moments, and she wasn't sure she wanted to remember it.

It hurt too much.

Hal's boots ground against splinters and glass shards. His shoulders under the blue sweater were absurdly broad, his hair was tied back just as it had been the last time she saw him, but his face was pale and drawn. And he held a squirming, kicking, very pale and thin man with lank dark hair up off the floor with one hand, the man's throat making little creaking noises as Hal *squeezed*.

The man—Cavanaugh, she remembered his name now—swung the glass-blade knife. It whispered through Hal's sweater, opening a long flapping slice of the wool. Cavanaugh's hazel eyes bugged out, and Hal tilted his head slightly. His free hand came up, and there was the ring, gleaming mellowly as Hal struck the knife away. It landed with a soft clatter somewhere in the hall, and Em realized she could breathe.

She could *breathe*.

Why is it so quiet? Am I in shock?

Hal's head turned. He glanced at her. Em choked, the retches shaking every part of her. Something had happened, and her body wasn't sure how to handle it.

Something's not right. I was...what happened? I was on the couch—

"Ohgod," May whispered. "Ohgod, Em, ohgod ohmygod..."

Em's lungs filled with air. Her hands moved when she told them to, no longer bound. Her eyes blinked. She ached all over.

He stabbed me, she thought, clearly and pointlessly. *Am I dead?*

"It's going to be okay," she whispered. "May? May, it's going to be okay. He's here."

Hal shook the man a little. "Fool," he said, quietly. "Was your long life spent waiting for this?"

Funny. Cavanaugh had looked so big when he was crouching over her, stabbing. Now he just looked like a broken-down old man.

Wait. He was young before. Or young-ish. He was aging as he hung from Hal's fist, withering in fast-forward. Lines branched from his eyes, poured from the corners of his mouth. His hair, still lank, crawled with gray, then white, then it began to slide free of his scalp in great clumps. He struggled, kicking, his face turning mottled-purplish, teeth losing their hold on his gums and popping free with small weird sounds.

May buried her face in Em's shoulder and moaned helplessly. Em sucked in another sweet, blessed, *clean* breath. "Hal." Her voice didn't want to work. Her throat was slick and hot with something that tasted so nasty just the thought of swallowing it made her stomach clench against itself. "Hal, *please.*"

"Do you hear that?" Hal said thoughtfully, to the melting, aging monster he held up. "I have finally found a bearer worthy of what was given me." He accompanied the words with a contemptuous little shake, and opened his hand.

Cavanaugh fell. He hit hard, with a snapping sound like old dry seasoned hardwood breaking, and Em winced. Breathing felt good. Breathing felt *marvelous*, and she had never before realized how wonderful it was and how much she wanted to keep doing it. Everything on her hurt, but she could *breathe*.

Hal turned on one heel, and in two swift strides was next to her, kneeling. "Emily."

She opened her mouth to tell him to be careful, someone had puked, but the vomit was gone. She lifted her left hand— her wrist was bruised, and her arm ached. "You..." She had to cough to clear her dry throat. He had her hand in both of his, warm hard skin and gentle fingers. There was a rattling behind him. Cavanaugh dug his wasted fingers into the carpeting, hauling his decaying body along. He was heading for the knife. "Behind...you..."

"Oh, God," May moaned into her shoulder. She wasn't

tied up anymore either, because she had her arms around Em. "Em, my God, don't be dead, don't be dead Em—"

"I'm not dead," Em whispered, and sagged in relief. *I'm not dead.*

There was another rushing sound, almost of water rippling under sunshine, and a cramp lancing up her left arm forced a small cry from her. Had she been stabbed after all, and this was death?

Hal leaned down close. He smelled of cardamom, of smoke, and of the night outside. His pupils flared, and his lips met her cheek.

"Rest," he whispered, and when he rose and turned, bearing down on the hideous thing still scrabbling across blood-soaked carpeting for its weapon, she closed her eyes.

❧ 45 ❧

HALF OF THE INFINITY

HER PHONE BUZZED.

Emily groaned, snaked one hand out from under the covers, and groped for it. Hal, anticipating, slid the small gadget within easy reach, and it disappeared under the covers. After a moment, a sleepy "'Lo?" came from under the blankets, and he suppressed a smile.

So strange, to feel his face move in such ways. Freedom was full of unexpected pleasures—and some very expected ones he could enjoy anticipating.

There was a muffled, excitable gabble from the phone's speakers. The redhead, he guessed, and cast a critical eye over her bedroom. It was just as it had been the first time he'd seen it, except bright thin winter sunshine slid its fingers between the blinds, striping the wall and giving the white paint a soft radiance. The rain was over, but there would be snow later in the week.

"Who?" She sounded half-asleep, still. Hal settled his feet again, cupped his hands, and the power took shape in his palms. "Oh, yeah. You're formally dating him?" Movement under the blankets. Hal's mouth had gone suspiciously dry. At least he was physical enough to feel it. It was…different, when he was not commanded to service a mortal woman for his bearer's edification or voyeuristic glee.

This felt much cleaner, and much more unsettling.

The mug in his hands warmed, and a whiff of coffee rose.

"May?" Much more awake now. "Are you okay? I mean—"

A tinny laugh, and if Hal chose, he could hear what the redhead was saying. In the end, he had decided the memories of Cavanaugh's attack were best erased from the woman's head.

"*Who the fuck are you?*" she had demanded, protectively clutching Emily's slack body, her blue eyes spitting fire. "*You leave her alone, or I'll—*"

Perhaps that was why Emily was her friend, and came so fiercely to her defense. Hal had much to learn.

"Okay, okay." Em sounded slightly more awake. More stirring under the blankets. He tried not to think of her legs, her trim little ankles, the soft slight weight of her in his arms as he had laid her safely in her mortal bed again. "Just…whoa. Bad dream, I guess."

What a mortal thing to say. The redhead's voice persisted, an interrogative tone to it.

"Oh, God, May." Em moaned, feelingly. "It's too fucking early for this. I'll call you back." The phone slid out, she pushed the blankets back, yawned…and froze, looking up at him.

Sleep-flushed cheeks. Her tumbled, glossy curls. That sweet curve to her mouth, even when it was ajar with shock. She stared at him, and her dark eyes were so wide she looked the beautiful girl-child she must have been.

"Fuck," she breathed, wonderingly.

He offered the white china mug tentatively. "I, ah." Every

word he had rehearsed for this moment fell away. "Um. I... coffee?"

Emily pushed herself up. No bruise or mark remained of Cavanaugh's visit. The nightgown was pale cream silk; it quite suited her. Hal suspected she preferred her own clothes to sleep in, but...he could not resist.

Nor could he resist bending down further. She did not move, staring at him, and when his mouth met hers, the pressure of lips did something strange to his ageless pulse. Filled every particle of his physical form with a light that had nothing to do with the invisible force used to work miracles. Her mouth opened, and he kissed her as he had seen mortal men do, holding the coffee awkwardly away.

It was not as the books described.

It was far, far better.

And over *far* too soon.

She blinked up at him, dazed and flushed. Shook her head, her mouth still slightly ajar, and he wondered what one of the heroes in those books would do now. Nothing seemed applicable except kissing her again, but he sensed once was all he was allowed at the moment. So he simply stood, and offered the coffee cup again, the handle turned carefully toward her.

Perhaps she thought it a dream and meant to rub at her face, to dispel sleep. Her hands came up, and she stared at the silver gleam on her left third finger.

It was not Hal's ring, safely fused to his *own* hand. This one was smaller, more delicate, but its stone echoed his. The claws of the setting on his were gentle flowerlike curves on hers, the band was thinner, but it vibrated with the same power his did.

What was half of the infinity he had been granted? Now he knew.

The smaller ring was wedded firmly to the flesh beneath, and Hal hoped she would not try to refuse it. "Forgive me." He found the words spilling out. "I left to deal with the Sophics, I did not think Cavanaugh could track you. I would not have left your side had I thought him capable of anything. Your friend will not remember, not even in her dreams, and you are safe. They shall not ever trouble you again. Nothing shall."

I will make certain of that, at least.

"Um." She studied the ring. Traced at its stone with one trembling fingertip. "Hal..."

Speaking again, to forestall her refusal. "I have shared half of what I am with you. I have done it without your...consent, and without your command. You freed me, and I—"

"Hold on a minute." She shook her head. "Okay? Just hold on one goddamn minute."

"Emily." He pitched forward, yearning toward her as the mortals had found planets yearned. If there was a gravity that could hold him, it was here in her small, messy bed, blinking at him in the light of a winter morn. "You cannot command me." He realized, miserably, that such a statement might well destroy whatever chance there was of earning her...what? Her regard? Her trust?

Something as numinous as the love the mortals craved?

"You cannot command me," he repeated. "But I will do anything you ask. *Anything.* Except leave you."

Her mouth closed with a snap. She glanced again at the ring. Traced the stone again, a small circular caress.

"Do I..." She caught herself. Darted him a wondering, troubled glance. "Do I grant wishes now?"

"Only one." *And that one is mine.* "Anything, Emily. Desire it, and it is yours."

"Oh boy." Emily's shoulders rose a little. "You're going to

have to explain *everything*." She lifted her chin, and her dark eyes shone. "Why don't you sit down, hand me that coffee, and get started?"

finis

ACKNOWLEDGMENTS

Thanks are due to Mel Sterling, as always; Miriam Kriss, who believed; and Skyla Dawn Cameron, who works miracles. A special shout-out to Holly Atkinson, who performed a yeoman's editing job.

Last but not least, dear Readers, thank you for once again allowing me to do what I love most: tell you a story.

Here's to many more.

ABOUT THE AUTHOR

Lili Saintcrow currently resides in the rainy Pacific Northwest with her children, dog, cat, and feral library.

www.lilithsaintcrow.com